P9-BVM-608

COUNTING TO PERFECT

Also by Suzanne LaFleur

Threads of Blue

Beautiful Blue World

Listening for Lucca

Eight Keys

Love, Aubrey

Suzanne LaFleur

COUNTING TO PERFECT

WENDY
LAMB
BOOKS

Text copyright © 2018 by Suzanne M. LaFleur
Jacket art copyright © 2018 by Ji Hyuk Kim

Visit us on the Web! rhcbooks.com

Educators and librarians, for a variety of teaching tools,
visit us at RHTeachersLibrarians.com

Library of Congress Cataloging-in-Publication Data
Name: LaFleur, Suzanne M., author.
Title: Counting to perfect / Suzanne LaFleur.
Description: First edition. | New York : Wendy Lamb Books, [2018] | Summary: Ignored by her parents since her "perfect" older sister, Julia, had a baby, Cassie, twelve, foregoes her summer plans to join Julia and baby Addie on a road trip. |
Identifiers: LCCN 2017049893 (print) | LCCN 2017058947 (ebook) |
ISBN 978-1-5247-7181-2 (eBook) | ISBN 978-1-5247-7179-9 (trade) |
ISBN 978-1-5247-7180-5 (lib. bdg.) | ISBN 978-1-5247-7182-9 (pbk.)
Subjects: | CYAC: Sisters—Fiction. | Babies—Fiction. | Runaways—Fiction. | Family problems—Fiction. | Automobile travel—Fiction.
Classification: LCC PZ7.L1422 (ebook) | LCC PZ7.L1422 Cou 2018 (print) | DDC [Fic]—dc23

The text of this book is set in 12-point Garamond.
Interior design by Trish Parcell

Printed in the United States of America
10 9 8 7 6 5 4 3 2 1
First Edition

To Mom and Dad
with l, a, & 20dc

Julia named her baby Adele.

Like the singer? everyone asked.

No, like herself, Julia said.

Not that we called her Adele.

Mostly we called her Addie.

Never *the baby.* Julia was very strict about that.

The other part of her name, the Cassandra part, that's after me.

But nobody calls me that, either.

I'm Cassie.

1

I woke to a weight on my chest, Addie's big blue eyes staring into mine. Her weight wasn't bad, sixteen pounds of snuggle baby. But it was bright in my room, so I shut my eyes and groaned about being woken up.

"Morning, Cassie!"

I peeked at Julia, hovering over us.

Never leave Addie on the bed! Mom must have said it a hundred times.

Not that either of us would. Julia always rolled her eyes about that. She rolled her eyes at a lot of what Mom said.

Julia was very careful. Way more careful than you would have thought from how much Mom reminded her of things. I guess that was Mom's job, to worry about everything.

Addie could sit up on her own, so Julia was letting her, but her hands were ready if Addie fell.

She didn't. She looked into my eyes and smiled, then let out a shriek. She noticed her bare toes in front of her and leaned forward to meet them, opening her mouth wide and *schlurp*ing on them.

"Aren't you excited?" Julia asked. "Soon you can just be with us, *all day long*."

My last day of school.

Julia'd hardly gone to school lately, but she'd gone enough, and graduated with her class two weeks ago.

Remembering her in her blue gown with red trim, her cap with the tassel, made a strange tickle in my throat.

I rolled over onto my stomach. Julia caught Addie in time, but she was still smiling.

They both were.

"Five more minutes," I said.

I went to the kitchen to get some orange juice.

My hand met Dad's, reaching for the fridge handle, too.

Probably getting milk for his coffee.

Dad paused, but not because of me.

He was looking at Julia's six A finals stuck all over the fridge.

First he looked proud, then he got tears in his eyes, then he looked proud again.

Nothing of mine showed on the fridge anymore. Not my portfolio poem from Creative Writing or my first-semester report card or my fifth-grade class photo from last year. Not for months.

Everything had been covered up by Julia.

"Morning, Dad," I said. "Um, I need the orange juice."

"Morning, Cassie," he said. Like he'd just noticed I was there. Even though our hands had been touching.

I grabbed the orange juice and poured a ridiculously large glass.

Let someone say something to me about it.

Not that anyone would.

I waited at the bus stop with my empty backpack. We hadn't had any homework, but they hand back so many things on the last day of school that I would need something to carry it all home in. The two other girls from my street, Carly and Elena, stood a little apart from me. They kept glancing toward my house.

I looked back. Julia was on our front lawn, holding Addie's hand high, making her wave goodbye to me.

I faced forward as the bus pulled up.

Carly and Elena were looking at Julia, though.

There were *some* good things about school ending.

I boarded the bus first and flung my bag into an empty seat. I sat down by a window that showed Julia and Addie, still watching and waving.

I folded my hands in my lap.

Julia's face fell, and she lowered Addie's hand.

The bus pulled away.

In the last five minutes of the day, our homeroom teacher handed out large, sealed yellow envelopes.

5

Everyone sat up straighter, ready to bolt.

Inside the packets: our report cards, summer assignments, and the names of our new homeroom teachers.

We were supposed to give them to our parents first—like that ever happened—and that's how they were usually labeled: *To the parents of so-and-so,* printed stickers with our student ID numbers and home addresses.

But my label was different—a name tag stuck over the official one. It said, *TO CASSIE,* in several colors of bright marker, and then underneath, very small, *(and her parents),* like parents were a sorry thing to have to mention and I was most important.

I looked around. Most of the labels were the official kind. There were a couple other colored ones, but not that many.

We were released; sixth grade was over. We poured into the halls. Kids tore open their envelopes. What were the teachers going to do about it, really? The kids cheered or groaned as they discovered their fates.

Seventh grade was done in blocks. Your English teacher was also your homeroom teacher, and then you moved through the day more or less with the people in your block, even if you split later for language or math. Finding out our lead teacher would tell us how much—or little—we'd see our friends next year.

I could have argued that I had a right to open my envelope, if a teacher caught me, because it was addressed to me, but I held it tight and beelined for the tree out front, where I had promised to meet Piper and Liana so we could open our envelopes together.

They were both there already.

"Ready?" Piper asked.

She and Liana ripped open their envelopes. Envelopes with plain printed labels.

They showed each other their homeroom teacher's name, and started jumping up and down and hugging. A match!

They stopped and looked at me.

"Aren't you going to open it?"

But I already knew.

My envelope didn't match on the outside.

I flipped it over and slid my finger along the seal, unclasped the metal prongs, slid out the papers.

Mr. Connelly.

I should have known. Julia had had him. She'd loved him. Like the label, everything he did was a bit more colorful than in the other rooms.

"That's okay," Piper said, after coming to check my paper. "Maybe we'll still have lunch together."

"Maybe."

Liana had moved on already, flipping through the summer assignment packet. "Book report on one of the books . . . letter introducing ourselves to our homeroom teacher . . ."

Again, my page was different. The book list was the same, but I wasn't asked to write a letter.

> Create a journal about yourself so that I can get to
> know you. Include memories or future hopes. You
> may choose a traditional text format, or explore

other media, such as a photo album, blog, or video diary. You will be graded on the following considerations:

—Clarity of presentation

—Apparent time spent

—How well I feel I know you after "reading"

Journals are due by August 29, one week before the start of school. You may drop off, mail, or submit by email, as convenient to the format you have chosen.

I liked writing projects okay, and usually did well on them. But my journal would probably be the most boring thing ever.

"I'll write my letter tonight," Liana said. "So it's done."

"I won't," Piper said. "Waste of time. Plus, you never know. Maybe something will happen to me over the summer. I don't want to have to do it again in two months."

"What would happen over the summer that would make things so different?"

Piper shrugged. "Want to go to my house?" she asked as we started to head toward the buses. We would have to take our own buses home, because we didn't have notes from our parents to switch, but we could meet up later.

"You could come to my house," I said.

Neither of them said anything for a minute, and Liana bit her lip.

"I can't," she said. "Sorry."

"It's not like it's contagious."

"Well, my mom, you know, she's annoying."

"Yeah, I know," I said.

Liana's eyes grew big.

"Sorry," I said. "I mean, I know it's annoying for you. Her rules."

Then her eyes narrowed.

"I'd come, Cassie," Piper said. "My parents don't care. But then Liana couldn't come, too. My house, okay?"

"Never mind," I said. "I think we're doing something anyway. Me and Julia."

Piper paused, and then she said, "Right. . . . So we'll see you at the pool tomorrow?"

I nodded.

Then we ran for our buses.

"Cassie, set the table," Mom said. "Dining room."

"Okay."

We ate in the dining room a lot. There was just more space.

I shoved Addie's high chair next to Julia's seat at the head of the table and threw a bib on it before I set out our four grown-up plates. I got four glasses of water with three ice cubes each, whether or not anybody was going to want them. I'd rather do that than get in trouble later for having done a lazy job setting the table. Then I sat and played a game on my phone. In three trips, Mom brought in a platter of chicken, a bowl of broccoli, and a huge salad.

Salad bowls. Crap.

I went to get them and the dressing bottles.

"Tell everyone to come for dinner," Mom said.

"Dinner!" I yelled.

"That's not what I meant."

I shrugged and slipped my phone into my pocket. We tried not to use phones at the table. The only call we'd ever take was from Carter, if he hadn't seen Addie that day.

Carter. Crap.

"Is Carter eating with us?"

Mom shook her head as she sat down and started putting broccoli on each plate. Then she reached for the chicken.

"White meat or dark?" she asked.

"I only eat dark meat." Why couldn't she ever remember that?

"That's right." She served me. "Where is everyone else?"

"Dinner!" I yelled louder than last time.

Dad showed up, and Julia with a sleepy-looking Addie. She must have just got up from her afternoon nap. Julia plopped Addie into the high chair and got a jar of baby food and a spoon.

Dad slid something across the table at me.

"Thanks!" I snatched up the entry tag for the local pool. Mine was green, for the first time. Under twelve is red, for "needs an adult." When you are twelve and get a green one, you can go on your own. So Piper, Liana, and I could just be dropped off, and stay all day, without having to get one of our moms to sit there.

"She had plums for lunch," Mom said to Julia.

Julia sighed and returned to the cabinet. "Sweet potato then."

"Sure," Mom said.

Julia came back.

Dad finished handing out the pool tags, all green.

"Addie's too young to need one," he explained.

"I might not need one either," Julia said.

"Don't you want to go to the pool?" Mom asked.

"Maybe. I don't know."

"You aren't eating." Mom put a piece of chicken on Julia's plate.

"I'm feeding Addie."

"Take a break, I'll feed her."

"No thanks," Julia said.

"Suit yourself," Mom said, but not like she was mad. "I think Addie would like to go to the pool."

"You take her," Julia said.

Nobody said anything for a few minutes.

"How was your last day?" Dad asked me.

"Super," I said.

"Really?"

I shrugged. "They put on a movie."

"Did you get your summer reading list?" Mom asked. "Julia, she's got that all over her hands now."

"It's on the fridge," I said.

"What?" Dad asked.

I looked at Mom. "My reading list. You asked for my reading list."

"Oh, that's right. We'll get you the books soon, okay?"

I nodded.

"What about a report card?" Dad asked.

"Hang on."

I got the envelope from the kitchen and handed it to him.

"Wasn't I supposed to open this?" he asked.

"It was addressed to me."

He flipped it over and checked. "Look at that." He slid the papers out. "Ah . . . Mr. Connelly. Here we go again."

"Oh, I liked Mr. Connelly!" Julia said.

"Julia," Mom said.

"What?"

"Just—watch her—I don't want her spitting sweet potato everywhere."

"What am I supposed to do about that?" Julia asked. "You'll like Mr. Connelly, Cass."

"I have a weird assignment already. To write a journal about myself."

"Oh, yeah! Mine's upstairs. In the attic. There's a box, it says *J Middle School*. Take whatever you want. You can't copy it, obviously. But some things will overlap, so maybe it will help."

"Thanks."

"Cassie should probably do her own entirely," Mom said. "Maybe she shouldn't look at yours."

"We grew up in the same family. Our stories overlap," Julia said. "At least she can see what a finished one looks like. I got an A."

"Of course you did," I said.

Julia raised her eyebrows at me.

Mom frowned, looking from one of us to the other. Then she made her I-give-up face.

Dad had been ignoring us, reading my report card.

"What happened in science?"

"Nothing." To be honest, I wasn't sure. A couple bad quizzes?

When he finally looked up, he said, "A fine report card. Well done." He handed it to Mom.

She looked it over. "Yes, that's nice. Well done, Cassie." She set the report card on the table.

I looked back and forth between them, waiting.

A good report card used to get me a sundae out. An excellent report card at the end of fifth grade and Dad took me to the bookstore with fifty dollars to spend.

All As this time, except the one B in science.

"Can I have something?" I asked.

"You want me to pass the chicken?" Dad asked.

"Salad?" Mom held it up.

"No, I mean for the report card."

"Oh."

"Oh."

They looked at each other, thinking with one mind through their eyeballs. When they did that, the conversation usually didn't turn out good for me. But Mom nodded, and then Dad said, "Sure. Sure, honey. Maybe . . . hey, why don't we go out to dinner? We could go tomorrow night. You can pick the place. How does that sound?"

"Everybody? Like, all of us?"

"Sure."

"You guys can all go out," Julia said. "I'll keep Addie home. Then you won't have to worry about her making a mess at the restaurant or needing to cut things short so she can go to bed."

"No," I said.

"Julia, you go, I'll stay home with her," Mom said.

"No," I said.

"I'm fine, we can stay home," Julia said. "It could even be nice to have a quiet night, just us."

"No."

Mom and Dad locked eyes again. But they weren't talking about me this time; it was like they couldn't even hear me. Like we weren't talking about my celebration at all. They were talking about Julia. Again.

"We don't want to leave you guys home alone like that," Mom said. "By yourselves. At night."

Julia stared at her. "What do you think is going to happen?"

"Forget it," I said.

"What do you think is going to happen?" Julia said again.

"Forget it," I said again.

Julia was glaring at Mom, who was looking sternly back, unblinking; they were having the biggest, fattest silent eye-conversation ever.

When did you learn how to do that? Nobody would teach me. Nobody would even meet my eyes.

Julia stood up, unbuckled Addie, still all covered in sweet potato, and sat her on her hip. Addie's eyes were big and a little confused, like she could tell people were getting upset.

But she was where she belonged, stuck to Julia, so she was still okay.

Julia and Addie left. Even though Julia hadn't gotten around to eating anything.

After a moment, Dad said, "You and me, kid. Anywhere you like."

"Forget it. I don't want to go."

He and Mom looked at each other again, but I don't know if they were eye-talking about me or about Julia.

"Something else then?" Dad asked.

"I don't want anything!"

"Why are you yelling?" Mom asked.

I threw my napkin onto my plate.

"I'm done, too."

Upstairs, the bathroom door was open, the light on.

Julia was giving Addie a bath. She had one hand on Addie's back; Addie was sitting up in the tub in a couple inches of water. She leaned forward, splashing her hands, smacking them into the water again and again when she realized she liked the splashes. Julia hadn't wiped the sweet potato off her face yet.

I stood in the doorway, not sure if it would be right for me to go in.

In the end, I just went to my own room and shut the door.

2

Julia brought Addie by for bedtime kisses, like every night.

She handed me Addie, clean of sweet potato and smelling like Johnson & Johnson baby shampoo. Then she sat on my bed, leaned against the wall.

The things we weren't saying hung in the air.

You okay?

You okay?

"You ruin everything," I said.

"Hey! Don't say that to her!" Julia sat up.

"I wasn't talking to her!" I looked at my sister. "*You* ruin everything!"

She blinked like she was confused. "Is this about your report card outing?"

"No! It's about *everything*."

"*Everything?* Since when?"

I studied Addie. Her bottom lip was sticking out.

"Are you sure you don't mean Addie?"

Like it would be somehow easier, if it was just Addie.

A squeezing heat grew inside my rib cage.

"Get out! Get out of my room!"

"What?"

"Go away!"

Julia didn't move.

"Go away, go away!"

"Fine!" Julia stood up and left.

Addie looked out the door after her.

"You forgot your baby!"

"No, I didn't!"

Addie had turned back to stare at me. She whimpered.

"Hey, hey, it's okay. It's okay. Sorry . . . I'm sorry." I turned her so she could lie down in my arms. I bounced her a little. She got comfy. Sucked on her fingers. Decided she didn't need to worry. But I whispered some more anyway: "I'm sorry, I'm sorry."

Julia came back for her later.

Addie being asleep was a good excuse for us not to say anything.

3

Another knock on my door.

"What?"

The door opened. Dad.

"Hey, kid."

"Hey."

"Look, I'm sorry about science."

I stared at him. Not the apology I was expecting. "What are you talking about?"

"I should have been paying more attention. I should have noticed. Been there. Could have helped you get ready for the final."

I stared at him. "That's . . . okay. . . ."

It was just a B. What was the big deal? It was a grade. Why did he care so much about my grades? He hadn't cared about much else about me over the past few months. But a bad grade made him freak out. Was I only grades to him? Were both of us?

He came and sat on my bed. Settling in for a longer talk.
Great.

"What?"

"If you're having a hard time with something, I want you to feel like you can tell me. Us. Me and your mother. Okay?"

"What are you *talking* about?" I tipped my head back against the headboard. Why had he even come in here?

"Why didn't you tell us you were having trouble in science?"

"Dad! I wasn't having trouble! It was just . . . boring. I got to the quizzes and didn't remember what I'd read the night before. That's all. I don't care."

"I care."

Then why didn't he care about the things I *wanted* him to care about? Why had he missed so many swim meets? Why had I missed April swim camp? Why hadn't he asked what I wanted to do for my birthday at the end of the summer, so we could plan it? Did he even remember my birthday was coming? Why hadn't he asked why Liana hadn't set foot in our house in months, and why me and my friends had to hang out other places?

"I'm tired," I said.

"Of course, it's late," Dad said. "Talk more tomorrow?"

"Mm." I let it look like I was going back to my book. He rumpled my hair—which I didn't like, but I tried not to pull away—and then he left.

I got up and paced, eventually settling on shifting pictures on my crisscross-ribbon bulletin board.

Maybe I could just mail the whole thing to Mr. Connelly as my project. He could analyze the layering, the pictures I picked to cover others—how that one of me and Julia at six and twelve was buried, buried, buried. How there were more swim medals from other years than from this past one, not because I wasn't swimming well, but because I'd had to miss so many meets. How there weren't even many new photos. How the whole thing looked kind of dusty and faded.

Apparent time spent: years and years.

But mindlessly. So it looked like I hadn't spent any time at all.

I hadn't known what I was recording.

I came to a swimming picture from more than a year before. Piper, Liana, our teammate Bea, and I, all in our black meet suits and red caps, smiling big smiles, even though some of us were still trying to catch our breath.

It had been a close meet—we were going to have to win almost every relay. But the other team was really good, and we rarely beat them at relays.

I'd had a great individual swim earlier—which hadn't prepared me for what Coach said as our relay team gathered behind the block.

"You girls get this, and the rest of our relays just have to not disqualify. Piper and Cassie, I want you to switch. Cassie, you're anchor."

I never anchored. Usually I led off to get us a great start, but to close the relay, you had to be so fast.

Whatever Coach said was what would happen. We couldn't argue.

"Okay, Coach."

"Okay, Coach."

"Safe starts."

All four of us nodded.

As he walked away, Piper said, "You got this."

I nodded, dancing on jittery legs, suctioning and resuctioning my goggles.

"Swimmers, step up."

Piper and the other first swimmers climbed onto the blocks.

Everyone went silent for the start.

As soon as the starter sounded, the crowd in the stands began to cheer.

After the third swimmers dove in, I climbed onto the block. Bea, good as she was, was losing our lead. If I knew I was going in ahead, I would know I could do it.

The cheering and screaming in the stands increased as the spectators stood. They all knew what was at stake. The sound filled the indoor pool, echoing, creating a wall.

It's easy to block out that wall.

My body channeled the sound into a useful ball of adrenaline beneath my rib cage. I couldn't hear it anymore.

In the silence I'd created for myself, I took a second to glance at the crowd and saw Mom and Dad. They weren't looking at me; they were watching Bea. Dad had his arms crossed over his chest; Mom, her hands clasped under her chin.

I looked back at Bea, heading toward me. In my peripheral vision, our competition pulled farther ahead.

I wasn't going to get a lead.

But it was only going to be a body's length they were ahead. If I had a great start . . .

I can do this anyway.

I pictured the adrenaline ball, packed it tight into a perfect sphere and wrapped it in a smooth white casing of calm, to save it.

No more jitters.

I stretched my arms out, steady, to follow Bea in.

As her hand extended to hit the wall, I dove.

One last millisecond of calm and silence as I hit the water, was truly alone but also carried somehow by my screaming teammates and our fans. I broke the surface and with it the adrenaline ball. Tingles hit all the way to my fingertips and toes. And then my arms were flying and my feet fluttering. I hit the turn without a breath—but that was okay, I didn't need one—and then I saw her, my opponent, hitting the wall at exactly the same time, creating another pretend split-second of calm stillness.

I got this.

I burst off the wall and stayed underwater longer than she did, and when I broke the surface again, I was ahead. I could see it, and I could hear it, because the crowd was screaming louder than ever.

I snatched a breath, because I needed one, but kept my head down after that. *Pull pull pull pull pull pull,* and there it was: I extended my hand and touched the electric timer three-tenths of a second before she did.

The crowd wouldn't stop screaming. Coach was jumping up and down. I climbed out, the arms of my crying relay teammates wrapping around me as soon as my feet had cleared the water, Piper squeezing me hard and Liana kissing me on my cap.

I looked at the stands: there were our parents, all tangled in a similar hug, other parents reaching to pat them on the shoulders.

I stood there dripping, unable to catch my breath, but it felt good, like I would *live live live* forever, my heart was pumping so fast and so steady.

Then we were walking, the four of us, back to the benches to grab our towels, the next relays getting ready.

But when we reached the stands, another round of cheering and applause had started. Our parents had rushed down to the front—a standing ovation—reaching to touch each of us, get handshakes and high fives. I swear Mom and Dad had tears in their eyes.

On the way home, Dad couldn't shut up.

"Cassie, that was . . . the way you just carried all of that, like it was no big deal, you were just so . . . confident."

Mom turned in her seat, put her hand on my knee, looked me in the eye. "Congratulations on a fantastic win."

There was another swim meet, about a month later but still before Addie, when we needed wins in the relays.

I was anchor again. Our relay started. We were a little be-hind, but I was going to get it.

Only I didn't.

My dive wasn't clean. My strokes didn't feel good; they felt short and choppy. I breathed a lot, and choked on water.

We lost.

I lost.

After getting in the car, Mom, Dad, and I just sat for a mo-ment.

Then Dad said, "That's all right. You'll get 'em next time."

4

The first official morning of my summer vacation.

I sat in a lawn chair in the front yard.

It was hot.

There was nothing to do before the pool opened. Mom would drop me off to be with my friends then.

Mornings at the pool: hang out; afternoons: swim practice with the team. Perfect plans for the summer.

I pulled my baseball cap farther down over my face. Maybe I could nap. Addie had woken me up in the night. Three times. And Julia had brought her in for her morning visit anyway. Even though we sat still and stiff and didn't say anything.

Someone plopped into the chair next to me.

"Hey, Cassie."

"Oh, hi Carter."

Carter visited every day. I guess he should have, because he was Addie's dad, but I was sick of him. It had been bad enough before Addie, when he was over every *other* day. It seemed like he got most of Julia's free time, and all of her smiles.

At least he had a summer job at the mall and then he was going to college. Nearby, but still, it would get him out of my space a little.

"I went to go inside, but Julia told me she's not ready."

Not ready? For what? She'd told him not to come inside?

I peered at him from under my cap.

"Hey, Cassie?"

"Yeah?"

"Is Julia . . . okay?"

"What do you mean?" I sat up.

What *did* he mean? Julia had had his baby when she was seventeen and he was asking if she was okay?

"Yeah, Julia's great." I settled back down in my chair.

"Oh, good, because, I thought you would know if something was wrong."

Why would I know anything? It wasn't like Julia told me things.

"You should check again. She's probably ready now."

"Um, yeah, okay, thanks Cass."

I did *not* like him calling me Cass. Only Julia got to do that. He'd heard her, but it didn't mean he was invited to.

I gave him a head start going inside, and then I trailed after and yelled, "Mom? Can you take me to the pool now?"

After a morning in the diving well, Piper, Liana, and I spread our towels on the concrete deck for our picnic lunch. My towel looked like a watermelon; Piper's had fat rainbow stripes.

Liana's was the faded *Finding Nemo* one Julia and I had given her for her seventh birthday. Probably the only thing left from that present, which had been her first swim bag, stuffed with gear like goggles and neon practice caps.

I opened my cooler: three bottles of water and one of sunscreen; a turkey-and-cheese sandwich; a whole bag of Goldfish crackers to share; three cookies, also to share; an apple. I'd packed the whole thing myself.

I tossed the sunscreen to Piper, who squirted some into her hands and came around behind me to do my back and shoulders. We each contributed one bottle of sunscreen for the summer—after a couple weeks of eight hours in the sun, we'd be so brown we wouldn't burn.

Liana picked up the bottle, gave it a squeeze into her hand, and knelt in front of me. "Your cheeks are pink already," she said, dabbing the sunscreen onto my face. She was so much more gentle than Piper, who was slapping me.

After we were all sunscreened, we tossed the food we'd brought to share into the middle. We laughed when Piper pulled out cubes of honeydew melon and Liana cantaloupe at the same time. Liana added a bag of baby carrots.

"Did you write your letter last night, dork?" Piper asked Liana.

"No," Liana said. "You know I didn't."

Then they both kind of stiffened, and took quiet bites of their sandwiches. I stopped eating mine.

"Why would she know?" I asked. "What happened last night?"

They looked at each other. Then Piper said, as if trying to get it over with, "We went to the movies."

I looked from one to the other.

"You said you had plans," Liana said. "We would have invited you. Of course."

Piper was nodding.

"Of course," I echoed. A minute ago, I'd been starving from swimming all morning. But my sandwich seemed dry and I slowed down.

I wanted to take my cookies back from the sharing pile.

I looked at our ankles, at our matching embroidery-floss friendship bands that Liana had made for us on the pool deck last summer. The colors were bleached by a year of chlorine, the threads growing thinner.

When it was time for swim practice, we gathered behind lane three with Bea, Sam, and Jordan. Our lane from last summer.

But then Coach came by and said, "Cassie, lane four."

Everyone in lane four was older than me. And really good.

You didn't argue with Coach, but I stood there for a minute, staring at Liana and Piper.

"Well," Piper said, putting on her goggles and meeting my eyes with her buggy ones. "I guess you're just too fast for us."

Piper's mom dropped me off at the end of the day.

When I got to my room, a huge pile of books was on my desk.

Brand-new, shiny, bright-colored science books, on a variety of subjects.

Barf.

I slid them all off the desk.

They made a terrific crash as they hit the floor.

I climbed the stairs to the attic.

The attic has a funny smell. . . . It's hot and stale, not air-conditioned, not lived-in. But Mom likes things neat. So almost everything is in labeled plastic bins, and she runs a dehumidifier to keep things from getting too damp.

The floorboards creaked as I crossed to where most of Julia's stuff was clustered together. Masking-tape-and-Sharpie labels said: *J Freshman Year; J Sophomore Year; J Junior Year.* No *J Senior Year* yet, but there would be.

Dad had insisted that Julia finish high school.

First he'd asked the guidance counselor if she could keep up with her homework and then sit her exams at the end of the year.

The guidance counselor said no. That, unfortunately, there was an attendance requirement. Julia wouldn't make it if she stayed home from Thanksgiving onward. Not to mention there was a physical education requirement and obviously that had to be done in person, too.

We all thought it was dumb. Even I knew that you don't learn anything during the school day, that you just sit there and get talked at and all the learning happens at home, when you do your homework. Julia was almost done with high school already. But if she was "homebound" for a while, a licensed teacher could visit her; that could happen for a few weeks after the baby came, and buy her some extra time. A doctor's note could get her three months of visits.

So Dad arranged that. He asked what the minimum number of days was and for a printout of her attendance so far that year. He figured out how many days were left for her to do after the home visits and when the PE classes would be. He built her this huge schedule on a calendar in the kitchen, with a few extra days here and there in case she got sick. And then he and Mom took turns using up their own sick days to be with Addie.

"I'll stay home with Addie," I'd offered one night at dinner, when everyone was discussing who would take a turn that week.

Dad looked livid.

Then he covered his eyes with one hand.

At first, I'd thought he didn't think I could take care of Addie.

But it wasn't that, not at all.

It was more like he'd never imagined that it would become so hard to get us through school. It had never been a question before Addie. His girls would go to high school *and* college. And then suddenly we were all struggling to get Julia a high school diploma like it was getting her to the moon.

So me missing school wasn't going to help anybody.

"I'm sorry," I said. "Forget it."

"That's right, forget it." Dad stared me down real good and hard and I swallowed and looked away.

"Thank you, Cass." Julia bounced Addie on her knee. "It's super sweet of you, but I would stay home with her before I ever asked you to. Ever."

I nodded. I cleared my plate and went upstairs to put in my earbuds and block them all out and do my homework.

I found *J Middle School.* I popped the cover off and sat on another bin.

Tons of projects. Photos. Study guides. Valentines. Notes. Pom-poms from pep rallies, ribbons from science fairs, itineraries from field trips.

Then a large, square, plastic-coated scrapbook: "A Photographic Journal by Julia Applegate." I pulled it into my lap and slowly turned the pages.

Not a word in the entire thing.

She started with her birth: her photo from the hospital.

I stared at the picture for a few minutes. She and Addie, as newborns, had the same nose. But Addie had more hair, a different chin.

Mom and Dad, looking so young, both with longer hair, bringing Julia home.

Feeding her baby food.

I flipped the pages. Preschool . . . Julia's friend Maya at three, then staying in the photos as Julia progressed through school.

Another baby.

31

Me.

I touched the photo of Julia holding me. She was kind of little, too, just six. Beaming at the camera with no front teeth. Then looking not at the camera, but at my face. Loving me already.

I flipped the page to find that I took over the album for a little while. My first Christmas; my first teeth; my fists wrapped around Julia's fingers as I walked with her.

Then I dropped back out of the journal.

Julia and her friends at Halloween. School assemblies. Birthday parties.

Our whole family at Grandma's at Easter. A smattering of the cousins we haven't talked to in a while.

It didn't feel like Julia had just stuck a bunch of random photos from her life in the scrapbook. She had chosen carefully; she told a story with characters in it.

I was there like a blip, a significant event at first, but then falling in with all the other characters. Or . . . falling off the radar.

I put the journal back into the bin and snapped the lid on.

I didn't know how to put together a project that good.

Before I could pull the cord to turn off the extra light, I saw another bin, a new one, labeled *A*.

Addie.

Had Mom made it? Or Julia?

I opened it.

Clothes Addie had outgrown. A few cards of congratulations Julia'd received, though there really weren't a lot of those.

Addie's ID anklet from the hospital. The booties, blanket, and hat she'd worn there.

I picked up pink newborn pajamas. I couldn't believe how much she'd grown already. The pj's looked tiny.

I held them to my nose, breathed in deep.

They still smelled like her.

There were a couple duplicates of her newborn photo.

I took one of them and walked back over and opened the *J Middle School* box again. I opened the photo album and placed the picture of Addie under the clear plastic on the inside of the back cover.

I shut the box, brought the journal down to my room, and put it on my desk in the space where the science books had been.

When I got downstairs, Maya was over. She took Addie from Julia like she was her own kid. She'd always been good with babies. They liked her.

Maya sat Addie on her knees and Addie stared up into her eyes, mesmerized. Then she saw Maya's frizzy hair and reached up to try to grab the wisps along her forehead.

"Did you have a good day?" Maya asked her. Not in baby talk. The way she would talk to anybody.

Addie studied her face.

"That doesn't sound too bad," Maya said, as if Addie had answered.

"What are you up to tonight?" Julia asked Maya.

"Remy and I are going to pick out our bedding," Maya said. "You should come."

Julia's smile faded. She didn't need dorm bedding. She was going to take night classes at the local community college in the fall. Going to college, but not *going* to college.

The last bedding she'd picked out had been for Addie's crib. She'd picked zoo animals over pink owls. She hadn't known that Addie was going to be a girl.

"No thanks," Julia said. "Carter's coming back later."

That didn't seem like a good-enough reason. They could be back in time for that, or leave Addie with him. Or maybe Mom and Dad and I could watch her so Julia could have some time with her friends.

Maya made a face like she was sad but understood, like she was trying to think of what to say, how to get Julia to say what she needed to say. Maya looked at me. I shrugged.

Julia stood and took Addie back. "I'd better give her her bath."

Maya smiled and stood up, too. "See you soon, pumpkin." She kissed Addie on the cheek. She paused and planted a careful kiss on Julia's cheek, too. "Tomorrow? We'll talk?"

Julia went upstairs.

Dinner was quiet, all the things it *wasn't* standing out. Not a celebration for a good report card. Not me with my friends, or Julia with hers.

Though Carter was over.

Carter held Addie in his lap and fed her a jar of peas. He kept her neat and tidy, and Mom had nothing to say about it.

"You guys should all come over this weekend," Carter said. "My uncles and cousins and everyone are coming for a cookout. They'd love to see Addie."

"Maybe," Julia said. "We'll have to see what we're doing."

We weren't doing anything. We never did.

"I think that sounds nice, Carter," Mom said. "Let us know when it is and we'll be there."

Julia glared at her.

I was doing the dishes after Carter left, when Julia and Mom started fighting about whether we should go to the cookout.

"His family should get to spend more time with Addie. He's her father."

"I understand he's her father. But I should get to be the one to say yes to things, not you. Maybe I don't want to go to a cookout this weekend."

"Why is this a big deal? It's a couple hours."

Was I included in the mandatory cookout attendance? Probably yes. They would say I had to go, to support Julia and participate in the family activity, and then not pay any attention to me once we were there. Maybe Carter would let me play on the Wii and stay inside.

Julia visited my room later, a sweet-smelling, pajamaed Addie on her hip. She handed me Addie and I played with her, but Julia walked in circles on my polka-dot rug.

"Cass?" she asked finally.

I looked up.

She stopped pacing and sat down on my bed. "Do you have any money?"

"Money?"

"You know, like real money."

"Do I have any money, like *real* money? What do you need money for?"

"Just, could you tell me?"

I bit my lip.

I was a saver. Everyone knew it. I'd pet-sat for every house in the neighborhood when people had gone on vacation last summer and at the holidays. And I hadn't spent my birthday money in three years.

Addie's eyelids had gone purple and puffy. She was getting sleepy. I turned her sideways in my arms to lay her down, and I rocked her.

"Don't you have some?" I asked.

"Grandma sent me a check for graduating from high school. Two thousand dollars—that's a lot, isn't it?"

"She must have been proud of you for finishing."

"Shut up. Nobody's proud of me."

"Everyone's proud of you."

"And I have some money, from before. It's like, maybe five hundred."

"I have . . ." I thought, but tried to keep my eyes from darting around the room to all the places I stashed my cash. "I don't know. I have something."

"Could I have it? Like . . . like a loan?"

I cringed, but cuddled Addie a bit closer.

"Is it for Addie?"

"Sort of. I mean, of course it has to do with Addie, but it's mainly for me."

I looked over at the journal on my desk. The science books all over the floor, open, pages getting creased.

"Please."

I looked into her eyes. She was begging. I couldn't tell what she was actually, silently, trying to tell me, but she really meant it, whatever it was.

"I'll pay you back. You know, when I can."

I sighed. "I'll think about it."

Julia nodded. Sat still for a minute. "Please?"

"I said I'd think about it. I don't know how much it is."

"Please."

I didn't like the way she just said please, over and over again like that.

But when I closed my eyes, I saw Mom's favorite vase, smashed at my feet.

Please, Julia? You won't tell, right? You won't say it was me?

Addie had fallen asleep, warm and heavy in my arms.

I looked at my sister, who was still looking down into her lap. "Why don't you just tell me what's wrong?"

"Nothing's wrong." She stood up suddenly, but was gentle as she took Addie. "Look, I better go put her down."

I wanted to hug her.

But Addie was in between us.

5

Whenever Liana and I slept over at Piper's, Piper slept in her big queen bed by herself, claiming she kicked, and Liana and I always slept on the floor in sleeping bags. I didn't know about Liana, but I never felt all that sleepy on the floor—eventually, I'd pass out from exhaustion, but I was always achy and tired in the morning. And cranky. Dad always said how cranky I was for days after sleeping at Piper's.

Piper never seemed to notice.

Once, when Addie was a newborn, I was at Piper's, lying awake. I didn't want to lie there anymore. I got up and went downstairs to the kitchen, got a cup of water, and sat on a barstool at the kitchen island. The clock on the stove said 3:11.

A little while later, the stairs creaked, and Liana came into the kitchen.

"You okay? I thought you'd just gone to the bathroom, but you never came back."

"Yeah . . . I'm just . . . not sleeping."

"Me neither."

Liana pulled out another stool and sat down.

We both stared at the box on the island.

Donut holes.

At my house, when we had sleepovers, Mom or Dad spent the morning making piles and piles of pancakes, with berries or M&M's or chocolate chips. Or if they were going to be busy, they bought a dozen all-different bagels with at least three kinds of cream cheese.

At Piper's, someone always left us a box of donut holes.

"Hungry?" Liana asked.

"Yes," I said slowly. I reached for the box, dragged it toward us. I opened it, finding that the donut holes were all the same: the squishy, glazed ones.

"My favorite," Liana said.

"Mine too."

Liana reached in, took one. So did I.

"Cheers."

We knocked donuts, stuffed them in our mouths, giggled.

Liana looked in the box again. "Let's eat them all."

"What will Piper have for breakfast?"

Liana looked around the kitchen, then pointed.

A box of Raisin Bran.

I giggled, took another donut. Liana did, too.

"We can pretend the box was never even here," I said. "We can hide it way down in the trash. So then Piper gives her parents a hard time about forgetting to get them."

We were both laughing. Liana grabbed my arm. "Shh! We'll wake everyone up."

We quieted down, reached for our third donuts.

"I kinda wish I were at home," Liana said. "At least then I'd be sleeping."

"I wouldn't be."

"The baby?"

"Yeah. She's up like two or three times a night. Screaming her brains out."

"Do you like her?"

I shrugged.

Liana licked her fingers thoughtfully. "You probably will."

"Maybe." I looked into the donut box. Took another. "You should come meet her. In the daytime."

Liana made a face. "You know my mom's not going to let me."

I kicked my feet on the rung of the stool.

"It's not my fault," she said.

"It's not *my* fault, either."

A couple donuts later, Liana said, "I think you must like Addie. If you want me to meet her."

6

When Julia came into my room in the morning, she set Addie on me. I rolled onto my stomach and pulled the pillow over my head, to show I didn't want to see them, that sleeping was way more important. Julia silently scooped up Addie and shut the door quietly as she left.

I fell asleep for so long it was after eleven when I got to the kitchen for breakfast.

"Where's Mom?" I asked Julia, who was drinking coffee and reading something at the counter.

"Work, silly."

"Where's Addie?"

"Sleeping."

I popped two pieces of bread in the toaster.

"I know you missed your ride to the pool. I can take you. It's Addie's long nap, though, so it might be a couple hours."

"Okay." I got the peanut butter from the cabinet. The oil had separated. I stirred and stirred, trying to get the peanut butter to look whole again. The way it was meant to. "Um . . . thanks."

"It's not a problem. I want to take Addie out today anyway, before Mom gets home. Maybe we'll go to the playground and try the swings."

Addie would probably like that.

Maybe I should have said the thought out loud. So Julia would know.

Not that she needed to hear what I thought. Not that she wanted to.

I started scraping peanut butter across the toast, letting the knife be noisy.

Julia watched me.

She got up, went to one of the cabinets, took out a jar. Set it by me.

Chocolate chips.

"Thanks." I sprinkled them on my toast, watched them start to melt.

"Maybe with something sweet, you won't be so grumpy-pants."

"I'm not grumpy-pants." I made a paper towel all soapy, to clean the oil I'd spilled down the side of the peanut butter jar.

Julia made a face like she didn't believe me. She went to the living room with her coffee and turned on the TV.

I stood holding my plate for like five minutes before I followed her. I sat next to her, our legs touching. I crunched my toast and then licked my fingers loud and smacky.

What's wrong? Julia didn't ask.

What's wrong? I didn't ask back.

Oh, nothing.

Really?

Yeah, sure, really. What would be wrong?

What do you need all that money for?

What do you *need all that money for?*

Do you like this show? 'Cause I don't.

Should I change it?

No, keep it where it is, so we can both suffer through it.

Okay, sounds good.

Julia's body never relaxed.

Neither did mine.

After two hours, Addie woke up and started crying.

Julia dropped me off at the pool an hour later.

Liana and Piper sat on deck along the fence. Had they wondered where I was all morning? Neither of them had texted.

Deciding to surprise them, I snuck up behind them on the other side of the fence.

"It's not fair," Piper was saying, "that she missed all those practices and meets, and she gets to move up a lane. I mean, do you think it's fair?"

Liana paused, and then said, "Is it not fair that she's better than we are, or is it not fair that Coach would reward her even when she hasn't been around?"

"Either," Piper said. "Both."

"Not really."

I didn't yell and surprise them the way I'd meant to. I ran away quietly, showed my tag at the front gate, and got ready for practice. I stood behind lane four. Liana smiled and waved at me from her lane, but I kept my hands shoved in my armpits, my eyes on the water.

I would show them who was better. I got in and swam so hard, but I swam harder than I should have to start out with. I got slower and slower.

"You all right?" Coach asked me.

"I don't think so."

"It's hot today. Get out and have some water."

Coach sent me home before practice was over. Which was good, because then I didn't have to talk to Liana or Piper. I said I was calling my ride, but I lied. I didn't want to explain to anyone why I wanted to come home early. It was only a couple miles, and I knew the way.

When I got home, no one was around. I hung up my swimming stuff, turned up the AC, and lay on the couch until I was freezing.

Still alone in the house, I wandered from room to room, seeing how they felt with no one in them.

Long drapes covered our dining room windows.

The drapes themselves have changed since I was little, but Mom's always kept something long and heavy.

I stepped behind them and stood there, almost hidden. I knew my feet would be poking out beneath.

When I was little, I made Julia play hide-and-seek all the time. Behind the drapes was one of my favorite spots. She always knew to look there, but she didn't even have to get close.

"I can see your feet!"

She would come over and pull back the drapes, and I would shriek.

"You hide! You hide!"

Julia was better than I was—she would hide completely behind a couch, under a bed, in a closet. Sometimes I had to look and look to find her. But I always did, in the end.

"Count! Count!"

We had picked thirty to count to. Ten was too short. Counting for this game was probably how I learned to count past ten in the first place.

Another favorite hiding spot was the bathtub, behind the blue rubber-duck-print shower curtain we used to have.

And in her bed, under her purple down comforter.

Once, finding me there, she climbed in and cuddled me, and we were so quiet and missing so long that Mom came to look for us.

But when Julia got older, she didn't want to play so much. Maybe she'd gotten tired of it, or maybe she was just busy. And I was getting too old for the game anyway.

I was eight the last time I'd asked her to count. She was already in high school, textbook and loose-leaf balanced on her knees while she sat up in bed.

"Please, Julia? Please?"

"One," she said.

I ran to hide, but stopped in the doorway and looked back. She was moving her pencil on the paper, writing the numbers of her math homework.

The moments beat past, but still, Julia was quiet.

"Why aren't you counting?" I asked.

"I am. Just . . . very . . . slowly."

She kept working. I waited.

Nothing.

She meant *very* slowly.

That Christmas, I opened a box labeled *To Cassie, From Julia* to find a small, flat card at the bottom with a very colorful *2*.

The next year, I came in third in freestyle in the finals at our regional meet. When Mom and Dad brought me home, there was a huge decorated poster board in the living room with a big number *3*.

"Isn't that sweet?" Mom had said. But she didn't really know what the number was for.

I'd flung myself at Julia.

The numbers had continued to come in slowly . . . for birthdays . . . written on napkins in my lunch on random days, with tempera paint on the tiles of our shower . . . arranged in Oreos on the kitchen counter.

Twelve in all.

But I hadn't gotten one for a long time.

Not since Addie was on the way.

Maybe a while before that.

I stood behind the drapes, the heavy fabric pressing on my forehead, my breath hot, trapped against my face.

No one said they could see my sneakers poking out.

No one was seeking me.

7

I went to my room and opened my desk drawer, rummaging until I found the wad of bills, rolled and held tight with a rubber band. I threw it onto my bed.

I slid my hands between the mattress and the box spring, finding more bills.

I went to my sock drawer, fished out the pair of fuzzy blue socks, pulled out the money I'd been hiding there.

Unpinned the twenty from my bulletin board.

Uncorked my piggy bank and shook it, carefully extracting the paper dollars.

I went to the closet and found the shoe box with the black dress shoes that were probably too small, yanked out the crumpled tissue in the toes.

Jackpot.

Where else?

My backpack.

My swim bag.

My jewelry box.

The lining of my winter coat.

Folded into my first-ever swimming T-shirt, which was too small but tucked in the bottom of my bottom drawer for safe-keeping.

I stared at the bills heaped all over my bed; then I sat and straightened them out, stacked them together from highest value to lowest.

Money. Like, *real* money.

I sat and held it in my hand.

8

Julia brought Addie in at bedtime, like always.

How lucky she is, Julia had once said, *to have her auntie right here all the time.*

Addie was looking super snuggly in pink feety pajamas, but she had a bib on to catch the drool.

She was always drooling. Her teeth were coming in. She had two on the bottom.

"We just had a bath," Julia said.

"Nice." It seemed like Julia was constantly giving Addie baths. I pulled Addie onto my lap and sniffed her head. "You still smell like a baby."

"Bad?" Julia asked.

"No." I sniffed again. "Good."

Addie was smiley, and when I caught her eye and smiled back, she squealed.

"She's so cute," I said.

"I know." Julia laughed. "You are," she said to Addie, in a baby-talk voice. "You are. You are *so cute.*"

Addie gurgled like she knew she was.

Bathing Addie had been such a big thing when she'd first come home. I didn't know, before that, that babies couldn't take actual baths, they had to be washed out of the water. Mom had given Addie her first bath at home while Julia watched—Mom had held her, head in one hand and body along her arm, in the bathroom sink, sponged her off, and cooed at her. Addie howled and thrashed around. Addie's second bath, Mom had had Julia do while she watched, me frozen in the doorway.

Julia wasn't comfortable. "She's so slippery," she'd said. Talking to Mom.

A few days later, when Mom was out, Julia interrupted me watching TV and said, "Come with me? I want to give Addie a bath."

"I don't know how to give Addie a bath."

"Me neither. But I'm going to figure this out."

I trailed upstairs after her.

"Sit," she said.

I sat on the closed toilet.

She handed me Addie.

Then she folded over a towel and made a cushion in the bottom of the bathtub.

She took Addie, undressed her, laid her down on her back on the towel.

Then Julia relaxed, holding herself way less stiffly. She sat back on her heels and smiled.

"There," she said. "Now I can't drop you, you squirmy little worm. And you can't fall."

She gave Addie a sponge bath.

She spoke only to Addie—not to Mom, who wasn't there, and not to me. I stayed on the toilet; she hadn't told me to get up. I might as well not have been there, either.

When she'd rinsed off the baby shampoo, she lifted Addie in a baby towel and held her against her chest.

Addie hadn't cried at all, not the whole time.

"Better go get a diaper on." Julia stood up. "Thanks, Cass."

But I hadn't done anything.

I reached under my pillow and pulled out a white envelope.

"Here." I handed it to Julia. "It's seven."

She opened the flap and saw the money.

"Seven . . . ?"

"Seven hundred."

"Seven *hundred* dollars?"

"Seven hundred twenty-three dollars."

Julia stared at me. "Are . . . you sure?"

"I wish you'd say what it's for."

"I . . . I'll pay you back. You know, when I can."

"Yeah, okay."

She put it in her back pocket and tugged her T-shirt down to cover it.

"Thank you."

Julia sat next to me, and though Addie was between us like yesterday, she leaned her forehead in to rest on mine.

I stared into her eyes.

"Cass?"

"What?"

"Addie and I are leaving tomorrow."

"Leaving?" I jerked my head and clunked hers.

"Ow," we said together, and both reached to rub our foreheads.

That's what we got for being so close.

"What do you mean, *leaving*?"

"I mean like getting in my car, and going."

"Going where? For how long?"

"I don't know. We just need to go."

I hadn't meant it, when I'd yelled *go away* at her. Not like that.

"You can't."

"Of course we can. Nobody's in charge of me but me."

"But what about Mom and Dad? They don't mind, about the baby. They'd rather you both be here."

"About *Adele*. They don't mind about *Addie*. She's a person, not a thing."

"I *know*. I didn't mean—"

"And I'm a person, too."

"Who says you're not?"

She was turning red. "Before you made me all mad, I was going to ask if you wanted to come with me. But you probably don't want to. So give Addie a good hug. A real hug."

"I always give her real hugs."

And I was. I was holding her to my middle so tight.

"But . . . come with you *where*?" I asked again. "Why don't you just tell me what's *wrong*?"

"You can't see what's wrong?" she asked, her voice getting higher. She wiped her eyes with the back of her hand.

Even though I was still holding Addie, I tried to hug Julia, too. She was stiff and didn't fall into the hug. Didn't let herself give it back. She got up and took Addie from me, though she wasn't even asleep yet like we usually waited for.

"I need to pack some things. You won't tell, will you? At least long enough to give us a head start?"

She stared me down.

I nodded. I pointed to Addie. Julia lowered her to me, and I kissed her pudgy cheeks, which were cool and smooth and also wet. She smiled at the tickle of the kiss, and I rubbed my finger over the same spot.

I looked up at Julia, wanting to touch her cheek, too, but then, she was gone.

9

One day in third grade, Julia met me at the bus after school. She met me every day, because Mom worked. But on that particular day, I held my backpack up to hide my face.

"Cass," she said.

"Yeah-huh?"

She grabbed my shoulder to stop my beeline for the house. Dragged my arm away from my face.

"Cassie!"

"What?"

"You know what! How did you get a black eye? Why didn't Mom tell me?"

"They didn't call Mom."

"They should have. I thought they always called your mom for things like that. Did you go to the nurse?"

"Yeah, for like an hour. They made me sit with ice. I missed math. Now I don't know how to do the homework."

"I can help you with the homework. So, how did you get that?"

"Fighting."

Julia froze, holding the door open for me.

"You got a black eye fighting and they *didn't* call Mom?"

"You should see the other guy."

"I think I got the wrong kid off the bus." Julia raised her eyes to the heavens, searching for answers in the sky. "Let's get some more ice on you. Mom isn't going to like this at all."

She took my bag and went to the kitchen for an ice pack.

"Who started it?"

"He did. He called me a bad name."

"What? What did he say?"

"Um . . . 'poopies.'"

She stared at me from the doorway to the kitchen.

"He called you *poopies*? You got in a fight over that?"

"No, it wasn't *poopies*. I just don't know a lot of bad words."

"That shouldn't matter if you remember what he said. Which you should, if it was worth a black eye."

She came back to me in the living room, pulled off my coat and dropped it onto the floor, and drew me onto her lap on the couch.

Sitting in the nurse's office had been awful, me leaning forward, holding the plastic bag of cold chemicals to my face, getting a headache and worrying about what I was missing.

But this was nice, with Julia. She smoothed my hair back from my forehead and pressed our soft freezer compress, cushioned with one of her own T-shirts, to my eye. I relaxed and leaned my head on her shoulder. Her fingers stayed in my hair, sending cool tingles down my scalp.

"Julia?"

"Hm?"

"The other guy was a chair."

"What?"

"I . . . I didn't fight anybody. I fell. In the cafeteria. I tripped and hit my face on a chair."

"Oh, Cassie . . . why didn't you just say that?"

She could feel the slight shrug of my shoulders.

"You were embarrassed?"

I nodded.

"Did everyone laugh?"

I nodded.

"Were you carrying your lunch tray?"

I nodded.

"So there was a big mess everywhere?"

I nodded.

"Did you get to eat anything?"

I shook my head.

"What a terrible, terrible day." Julia held her hand against my forehead and then my cheeks, the way Mom did when she checked for a fever. Except Julia was way more gentle than Mom.

"It was spaghetti day."

"Your favorite."

Through my good eye, I had seen the spaghetti spattered all over the floor. And I had been so hungry.

Julia wiggled to get her phone out of her pocket. She swiped around a little, put the phone to her ear.

"Yes, this is Julia Applegate. I would like to speak to the principal. Now, please. . . . Regarding? My sister came home injured. . . . Thank you."

Julia was quiet again for a few minutes; then she exploded.

"Yes, hi. My sister Cassie came home from school with a black eye, of which we were not informed. I was under the impression it was school policy to call the parents in the event of any injury to the head. Furthermore, my sister informs me that she was injured during the lunch hour and no one thought to see that she had anything to eat. This is unacceptable. . . . Yes. . . . Yes. . . . Not at all. . . . No. . . ."

For the first time in hours, I smiled.

"I would consider this negligent, wouldn't you? What if my sister had needed to see a doctor immediately? . . . Yes. . . . I don't think so, not at all. . . . I'm sure you will be receiving another phone call from my parents, and possibly a message in writing. . . . Yes. . . . Goodbye."

Julie ended the call.

"You have my school's number in your phone?"

"Yeah. Mom put it in there. In case you weren't on the bus one day."

"You were awesome. You sounded like a lawyer."

We rested in a heap for a few more minutes, until the ice pack went warm.

"I'll make you some spaghetti."

"Really? In the afternoon? What about dinner?"

"Who cares. I'm sure you're hungry."

"Can you put meat crumbles in it?"

58

"Meat crumbles? I guess, if we have some, I could figure that out. Might just not be as disgusting as in the cafeteria."

"It's not disgusting."

"I know, pet. I know." She nuzzled my cheek with her nose, and I turned and kissed her. She set me on my feet.

While we waited for the pasta water to boil, I sat on a barstool at the kitchen counter, and Julia stood across from me, patiently teaching me the math I'd missed. By the time Mom came home, I was swinging my feet, happily working on a huge bowl of spaghetti and meat sauce.

"What's going on in here?"

"I made Bolognese."

"You can make Bolognese?"

"I just followed the recipe. It was easy."

"Well, I guess we can all eat that. It smells good." Mom leaned in to kiss me but paused, her hand under my chin. She turned my face, studying my eye. "Is there something else you girls want to tell me?" She looked at Julia.

She probably thought Julia and I had been fighting. She probably thought Julia had made dinner to make up for it, to dig herself out of trouble. She probably thought she needed to get me a different sitter.

"She got off the bus like that. Fell at school. They didn't call you, but I called them and the principal is expecting an irate call from you later." Julia met Mom's eye with a funny, tight smile.

Mom nodded. "I'll do that. Homework?"

"Cassie's is done; mine's barely started, and I have a bunch of proofs due tomorrow."

"Go, darling. Thank you."

Julia set up in the dining room.

I found her there, hours later, still working. I climbed into her lap, and she rested her chin on my head, not even interrupting her concentration as she copied things from her math book onto her paper.

"Your math looks different than mine."

"Yes."

"What are you supposed to do?"

"You list things you know on one side, and the reasons you know them on the other."

She didn't want to talk, so in my head I listed the important thing I knew, and the reasons I knew it:

Afternoon cuddles. A brave phone call. An hour spent making Bolognese. Doing my homework first.

I stayed put in her lap until Mom came to tell me it was time for bed.

10

I heard them.

I guess I'd never really gone to sleep. I'd tossed and turned and twisted my blankets around and around.

But I heard her up with Addie. I heard her come out of her room and shut the door.

It was clever, really. . . . She could be up with Addie at any time. Unless things sounded seriously wrong, like Addie wouldn't stop shrieking, Mom and Dad let them be. Not like when they first came home and Mom and Dad got up with them all the time and I hid in my room with a pillow over my ears.

Julia came back to her room a couple times.

Then the front door opened downstairs. She seemed to be going in and out of that, too.

I went to my window, trying to peer out, but I couldn't see them.

I stood at the window, frozen.

Then I grabbed my duffel bag. I reached into each of my dresser drawers just long enough to grab a fistful of whatever was there. Undies. Socks. T-shirts. Shorts. I yanked on jeans and pulled a sweatshirt over the T-shirt I'd been sleeping in. I snatched the pillow off my bed, grabbed my phone, strapped the bag across my chest, and ran—but quietly, quietly—down the stairs. I dragged the front door shut behind me and ran to the driveway.

I stood there, panting.

Julia turned in the driver's seat to look behind her before backing up.

She saw me, standing there.

We looked at each other.

Then she leaned toward me, reaching all the way across the car to open the passenger door.

I hopped in.

11

I woke to sunshine, a stiff neck, and Addie whining in the backseat.

"Morning," Julia said.

I squinted out the bright window.

Where were we?

"She's hungry," Julia said.

That was all? That was all she had to say?

"Are you going to feed her?"

"I'll have to. You, too, though; you'll be hungry. Ready to stop for breakfast?"

She sounded like Mom.

Or at least, *a* mom.

Which she was.

"I'm going to look for a diner," she said.

Addie took her wailing up a notch.

"It's too bad she still nurses," I said. The driver was the only one who could feed her.

"Too bad? It's terrific. She's not going to cost anything to feed. Maybe just some jars of baby food, like fruit or something. Squash maybe. I'll get some when I see a grocery store."

I didn't see any grocery stores out the window. Just trees. We were on a highway. Julia pulled off where there was a sign with pictures of a knife and fork, a bed, and a gas pump. At the end of the ramp was a street with a diner.

She stopped the car and got out, but she didn't go into the restaurant. She climbed into the backseat, unbuckled crying Addie, and started to feed her.

What are we doing here, Julia?

"You don't want to do that inside?" I asked, my stomach rumbling.

"I don't want people asking questions."

"Oh . . . hey, did you leave a note?"

"A note?"

"At home. Did you leave a note?"

"No. Did you?"

"No. There wasn't time."

Julia watched a couple headed into the diner. "I didn't know what to say."

"Won't Mom and Dad be worried?"

The answer, of course, was *yes,* but talking about it was going to be an even bigger waste of time than asking where we were going.

"Did they call or text you?" Julia asked. "Where's your phone?"

I dug into my duffel bag and pulled out my phone. Ten texts from Dad. I scrolled through them. "Um, Dad asks where we are. Then later he's just like, 'hope you're having fun.' I think he's decided we're just out for the morning."

"Text him back. Text him back and say . . . say, 'Yeah, be home soon!'"

Be home soon, I wrote.

Be home soon.

"That's a lie, though?" I asked.

Julia switched Addie to her other breast.

"You feel bad about it?" she asked.

Do I? I thought as a breeze blew in my open window and played with my hair.

It was nice out. Green and vacationy. Everyone at the rest stop was on vacation. No one else was running away.

Was that what we'd done? Run away?

I looked in the backseat at my sister and her baby. Julia looked tired, but relaxed and also . . . something else.

"No," I said. "I don't feel bad."

My stomach rumbled, and after a little while Julia pronounced Addie finished. She burped her, and Addie gurgled, happy.

"Get my bag?"

I grabbed her purse from the floor and slid out of the car as she got out with Addie.

We went into the restaurant. Since Addie could sit up, Julia said yes to a high chair and lined it with a blanket around the front to make it softer and keep Addie from getting germs.

"Do you think they think all three of us are sisters?" I asked when the hostess had walked away.

"I don't care what they think."

Well, that wasn't true. If it were, she wouldn't have been breast-feeding in the car.

I pulled one of the huge plastic menus in front of me.

"Go easy on the grub," Julia said. "Not like a lumberjack breakfast. You don't need all that. Something cheaper, like two eggs and toast or something."

My teeth clamped together for a second.

"What?" she asked. "What's the matter with you?"

"Aren't we here on . . . my money?"

"We have a . . . combined pool of money. Which I'm managing."

I did the math in my head. "Don't we have like . . . three thousand dollars? More than that?"

"Yes, but no way to replace it, when it runs out."

"How long are you planning to be out here?"

She didn't answer.

"And why are *you* managing the money? I'm a better saver than you. You should let me do it."

"Because I"—she raised an eyebrow over her huge, stupid plastic menu—"have a high school diploma and you don't."

It took the pause of a moment, and I don't know which of us started it, but we laughed. It sounded like such a small, ordinary thing, but getting her that diploma had been a daily crisis for our whole family. We laughed and laughed, and when the waitress came over we were still laughing.

"Can I get you girls something?" She was smiling, but she looked a little like she wished we weren't making so much noise.

"What the heck, we'll share a lumberjack breakfast, eggs over easy, two plates. And you have those little boxes of cereal? Can I get one of Cheerios?" Julia looked at the waitress sweetly. She sounded like such a grown-up, ordering like that. She handed over our menus like she ate in restaurants every day.

The waitress brought the Cheerios first. Julia put a few of them on the table for Addie to try to pick up and gum.

"That should keep her busy for a while," Julia said. She put the box in her purse. "Maybe this afternoon you can give her the rest in the car."

Where are we going?

The waitress brought over the drinks that came with the lumberjack, which were a glass of orange juice and a refillable mug of coffee. Julia pushed the juice in front of me and kept the coffee for herself.

That was smart. Maybe she would be a good manager of our money after all.

"Where are we sleeping tonight?" I asked.

"How about a hotel? One with a pool?"

"A *hotel* with a *pool*?"

"Why not?"

"What is that, like a hundred dollars?"

"Something like that?"

"Julia . . ."

"Calm down, okay?"

"Yeah, yeah."

"Have fun, okay?"

Was that what this was about, having fun?

The food came. Two eggs and two pancakes and two pieces of toast and some bacon and ham and sausages. So much food.

"We won't even need to get lunch," Julia said with a smile. As if that had been part of her money-managing plan the whole time.

We got back in the car and we drove.

Or, well, Julia drove. Obviously.

I looked out the window.

Addie looked out the window.

Addie fell asleep.

I didn't.

"What do they say about me?" Julia asked.

"Who?"

But I knew who she meant of course.

Everyone.

My friends.

The other kids at school.

Their parents.

Rude grown-ups.

The whole wide world.

"You can tell me. I can guess already."

I wiggled my toes in my wearing-out sneaks and pressed

the button for my window to go up and down. I took the hair tie out of my hair and shook out my ponytail and then made a new one, high and tight. I risked a glance over at Julia, and she looked mad, defiant.

But she was the one who'd started the conversation. She must have wanted to talk about it.

"How . . . how *did* Addie happen? I mean, that's mostly what people say. That there are things you can do to, you know, *not* have a baby."

"So they say I'm stupid?"

I didn't answer.

When she didn't say anything else, either, I offered, "It's been hard for me too, you know."

"Oh, poor you."

"Julia—"

She looked over at me, managed to smile. "No, I know. It's okay. I'm sorry." A few minutes later, she said, "How Addie Happened . . . ," like it was the title of an English essay. "There are things you can do, and we were doing them."

"So you weren't being stupid, it was really an accident?"

Her eyes flicked up to the rearview mirror, then took in Addie in the mirror over her car seat.

"I don't like that word anymore. I prefer *surprise.*"

We sat in silence for a few more minutes, listening to little Adele Cassandra's soft but steady breathing from the backseat.

Why had she named her daughter after me? And why had she wanted to invite me along on her silly car trip to nowhere? She could have brought Maya or Carter. Someone she wanted to be with more.

"We're going nowhere, aren't we?"

"I hope not, Cass. I hope very much that we're not going nowhere."

The sky was suddenly overcast. It poured for five minutes straight, and then, just as suddenly, it was sunny again.

"Does *surprise* mean you wouldn't go back and change what happened? That you're happy Addie is here?"

She looked up in the rearview mirror again. I turned in my seat to look at Addie's mirror, too. Addie was sleeping, with her head drooping, a light trail of drool sliding down her chin and making a puddle on her bib.

"I wouldn't trade Addie for anything."

12

I'd gone to the hospital to meet Addie.

With that jittery feeling like when I had to speak in front of the whole school or when I had to tell Mom or Dad I'd lied about something. Like I had to be torn open raw and put up for everyone's judgment.

Mom had stayed at the hospital; just Dad came to get me.

I was very quiet in the car, squeezing and squeezing the door handle.

"You all right?" Dad asked.

"Hm." I fiddled with the knob for the radio, looking for a new station, but nothing seemed good.

After a minute Dad said, "You know a baby can hear the people around it when it's still inside its mother? That it knows them by their voices?" He glanced over at me quickly and then back to the road. "She already knows you. She's wondering where you are."

She's wondering where you are.

"And our Julia, she's still our same girl. She's tired, but you'll see, your sister's okay. I know the hospital is scary, but that's our family over there; it's important that they see you, that you're there to support them."

Mom and Dad, and even Carter, let me go in to see Julia alone.

I don't know if that was something they'd talked about doing, or if Julia had asked them for it, or if they were just trying to keep things calm in her room. Maybe there was a rule about how many people could visit at once.

I stood in the doorway, clutching the strings of five shiny pink Mylar balloons and a soft white bunny with a pink bow.

"Come in, silly," she said.

I went over to the bed and stared at the little pink-faced creature—mostly just a nose poking out between a hospital blanket and a newborn's cap—that lay in the clear bassinet next to Julia's bed.

"What do you think?" she asked.

"That came out of you?"

Julia laughed. "One day very soon, you are going to be too old to get away with stuff like that. Just saying. Really, what do you think?"

"I don't know."

"Pick her up."

I knotted the balloon strings at the end of Julia's bed and set the bunny on the spare chair. I lifted the baby.

We'd learned how to pick up babies in Julia's classes. They were whole-family classes, for expectant teen mothers and their families, about baby health and hygiene and safety. There'd been a ton of baby dolls, and we'd had to learn how to hold them and change them and pretend-burp them and all that kind of stuff. Two hours, every Saturday. I'd never got out of a single one of them.

You have to be supportive, Mom had said. *You have to show her you are getting ready for this baby, too.*

Even though while everyone was getting ready for this baby I'd missed three swim meets, and the ones I'd made it to did not have a lot of spectators cheering for me.

Supportive.

Support the newborn's head.

I slid one hand under little Addie's head and one under her back and I lifted her while Julia watched me closely.

Why was she trusting me so much?

I looked at Addie, who didn't even wake up.

"Here." I handed her to Julia. She looked surprised that I didn't want longer, but she took Addie into the crook of her arm all the same.

"She likes you," she said.

"She doesn't."

"She does, I can tell."

I looked at the IV needle and tape on Julia's hand. What was that for? Her skin was bruised. She had purple circles under her eyes.

Had it been awful? Did she scream and scream and tell Carter she hated him, like on TV? Had Carter even been in the room?

My sister had had this huge thing happen in her life, and she had been strong and brave like a grown-up. I dropped onto her bed, feeling so small.

Julia reached for me with her free hand and rested it on my leg.

A nurse came in.

She was nice, just like you might picture on a baby ward. Her scrubs had pictures from *Curious George Goes to the Hospital* on them, and she was plump and fluffy-haired and smiley.

"Are you the proud auntie?" No hint of her thinking it odd that I was twelve and the proud mama only seventeen. That maybe we weren't proud. That maybe we were a hundred other things, like ashamed and scared and trying to be supportive.

"This is my sister, Cassie," Julia said.

The nurse took her temperature and blood pressure and said everything looked good and it was probably time to feed the baby again.

Julia said, "Can't I give her bottles?"

"We encourage all our mothers to breast-feed. Let's just try it again, okay?"

Julia exposed a boob, like I figured she'd been shown to do earlier. I'd never actually seen my sister's boobs. There hadn't been a reason to see them. I was surprised she even had enough boob to feed a baby. The nurse seemed to think it was all okay though. She touched my sister and Addie gently here and there while Addie tried to eat, as if it were a totally normal thing to do. I sat stiff on the bed, waiting for it to be over. Was this going to go on all day at our house now?

The nurse went to take care of something else for a few minutes. Julia reached for my hand and placed it on Addie's little back. I rubbed it.

"She does like you," Julia said. "I can feel her relaxing."

Could Julia feel that I was doing the opposite of relaxing? That my hand tensed against hers and wanted to pull away?

The nurse came back and helped Julia burp Addie. That was the best view I got of her smushy little face, when Julia held her up that way. The nurse showed her a couple ways to try until they got a good burp.

"Come along, Aunt Cassie," she said. "I'm teaching your sister to breast-feed, and we think that's best, but I'm going to teach you to make a bottle, just in case. You never know when you might need to help."

13

As promised, after two more stops to breast-feed and one to refill the gas tank, Julia pulled off the road and found us a hotel with a Vacancy sign and a pool.

My phone beeped again. "What should I say to Dad? Won't they worry when we don't come home tonight?"

"Say . . . say whatever you want."

Julia asked about a room while I sat outside the front door with Addie in her car-seat carrier and our four bags of luggage. She returned after a minute with room key cards. She slung a bag onto her back and picked up Addie, and left me to drag the other three bags.

Our room was a typical hotel room. We each got our own queen bed, and there was space for Addie's Pack 'n Play.

We jumped onto the beds right away, as if we were any two girls out on a family vacation.

"You want to go in the pool?" Julia asked.

"I didn't bring a bathing suit."

Julia stared at me, her mouth open. "You're a swimmer. When does a swimmer ever go anywhere without a bathing suit?"

"I forgot."

"You *forgot?*"

"Well, I was in a hurry and didn't know where we were going or what we were doing or how long we would be gone!"

Julia could tell I was getting mad, so she threw a balled pair of Addie's tiny socks at me. Addie's eyes followed them across the room and she laughed when they hit me.

"Is that funny?" I asked her.

"You can have one of my bathing suits."

"You brought bathing suits? So *you* were planning on swimming?"

She opened her suitcase and tossed me a bikini.

"I'm twelve. I can't fit in this."

"Who cares? I bet you brought a T-shirt the size of a tent you can wear over it."

True, of course.

Julia had a surprising amount of baby swimming stuff for Addie. Mom must have bought it. Special diapers and a cute white-and-red-striped bathing suit with frills and a white sun hat with a chin strap and baby sunblock that was like SPF 80. Julia insisted I put the sunblock on, too, and I did, but I didn't like how it made me all creamy and I couldn't seem to rub it in properly.

"That is some bathing costume," Julia said, glancing over at me.

77

"Shut it."

When we were all changed, which took like half an hour, we headed out to the pool.

There were other families there, though none of them looked as unusual as we did.

Maybe I had to stop thinking of us that way, as all wrong.

Julia claimed a table with an umbrella and some chairs so she could sit with Addie in the shade. I rolled my eyes, thinking of all the bother we went to with that sunscreen.

"You coming in?"

"In a minute. You go ahead. Don't you want to do your laps? Aren't you missing practice?"

After yesterday, I wasn't.

"It's not that kind of pool. Plus, I'm in this ridiculous outfit that's pure drag."

"I thought you guys liked that kind of thing. I thought that's why you wear ten bathing suits at once."

I shook my head at her. Julia had just never understood about swimming.

But that being the same about Julia, the same as it always had been, was enough to make me smile before I ran to do a cannonball.

Later, Julia picked up Addie and waded out to me in the water.

"Are you forgetting?" she asked. "It's baby's first swim. I think her Auntie Cass should do the honors. She is, after all, a professional swimmer."

"Really?" I tried to retie my ponytail without flicking water all over their faces.

"Of course, really. I'm right here. There's a lifeguard. Go for it."

Julia handed me Addie. I started by just dipping her toes in the water. She kicked twice, then stretched out tall and made a happy face. Slowly, I moved her back and forth, back and forth, lowering her a little bit more, and she kept smiling. Finally I had her in to her armpits, and then I started walking backward. Her feet floated up behind her.

"Wow," Julia said.

"What?" I asked. "Kicky, kicky. Kick, Addie! Kicky, kicky."

She did. She laughed. I laughed.

"You just like, know the water. How did you know what to do?" Julia asked.

"I just did what felt like the right thing to do."

Julia watched me drag Addie around the pool.

"You know what else I want to do?"

"What?"

"Dunk her."

"Dunk her? Like, underwater?"

"Like underwater."

"Is that safe?"

"The lifeguards do it to the babies in the swim classes at the pool. Like this, see?"

I blew in Addie's face. She scrunched up, and I dunked her just for a second. She looked surprised, but I was holding her so tight and so steady that she probably only thought the water splashed her in the face and not the other way around. She sputtered and opened her mouth wide. She wasn't smiling anymore, but she wasn't freaking out, either.

Julia looked like she'd had a mini heart attack, and then she recovered enough to laugh. She looked at me, like she wanted me to explain.

"Coach says we're all born knowing how to swim. We *forget*. We forget and then someone has to teach us all over again like we never knew."

"But then—"

"Yeah." I handed Addie back to her mother. "But then the second time, your body *never* forgets."

Julia studied me for a minute, like she was considering something she'd never thought of before.

"You know what else Coach says we're all born knowing and that we forget?"

"What?"

"How to climb like monkeys! *Ooo ooo ooo ooo!*" I climbed monkey fingers up Addie's arms to her chin and she squirmed to block my tickles. Then I threw myself backward in an arc and swam around them underwater to pop up on their other side. Addie shrieked.

"Cass!" Julia said.

"What?" I asked.

Had I splashed her?

Made her mad?

"Cass," she said again, waiting for the water to drip out of my ears, waiting for me to really listen.

"What?"

"This is the best day I've had in a long time."

I smiled. "Me too."

"Hey, what do you want for dinner? You pick. Anything you like."

Mom's chicken parm. But I couldn't say that. Not with Julia out of our parents' house having her best day ever.

"Burgers. And heaps of french fries."

"Done," Julia said. "Perfect after a summer swim, don't you think?"

"I do. That's why I suggested it."

She and Addie played in the water and watched me as I did rings of perfect, smooth, unbroken dolphin dives all around the pool.

14

At bedtime, I took out my phone.

Dad had texted us a bunch more.

I texted back: We're going to have a sleepover. Girls' night out.

Dad: Everything okay?

Me: Yeah super

Dad: You have somewhere to stay?

Me: Yeah

Dad: So . . . we'll see you in the morning.

Me: Tomorrow night

Dad: ?? Okay . . . you guys are together and okay?

Me: YES!

"That Dad again?" Julia asked from the other bed.

"Yeah. He's worried." Probably Mom was, too. So worried she didn't even know what to text. Did we have diapers? Were we eating? She was probably asking Dad to talk to us and trying not to freak out.

Julia came and took my phone from me. She turned it off and tossed it into my duffel bag.

"That's part of our vacation, okay? Just girl time."

"Yeah, okay. . . . I told him we'd be home tomorrow. We will, right?"

Julia sighed, got in her bed, and turned out the light.

In the morning, someone was wrapped around me.

"Julia, what are you doing?"

She stretched, letting me go.

"Oh, I don't know."

"Don't you have a baby to cuddle?"

"Yes, I do. But she's sleeping. She was up in the night."

"Yeah, I noticed."

"I think it's her teeth bothering her."

"She doesn't have a lot of teeth *to* bother her."

"Sure she does, they're underneath her gums, sawing their way through."

"Ouch, Julia!" She'd run her fingernail across my arm.

"Shhhh, don't be so loud—do you want to wake her?"

"Too late."

Addie didn't sound upset though. She was cooing happily.

"I like that sound," Julia said, burrowing back into my pillow.

"Me too," I said.

An hour later, with Addie changed and fed and dressed in fresh clothes, Julia said, "Pack."

"Don't we like it here?"

"We do. But not enough."

"So we're going home?"

"Nope."

"But . . ."

She glared at me.

"But I told Dad we were coming home." My voice was tiny.

"'But I told Dad we were coming home,'" she mocked, sounding even whinier.

I probably deserved that.

"Well," I said, trying to sound more confident, "I did say by tonight. So we have until then."

I scooped all my things into my bag. I left the still-damp bikini in a wad in the outside pocket. I could spread it out in the car.

"Leave your phone in there. I don't want to see you turn it on today."

"I probably can't. You have the only charger and I haven't plugged it in. . . . Julia?"

She was organizing her many bags—the diaper bag, her bag, Addie's bag.

"I didn't bring a toothbrush."

"You didn't?"

"No, remember, I was in a hurry to catch up."

"Why didn't you say that last night?"

"I didn't think of it last night."

"You didn't think of brushing your teeth before we went to bed last night?"

"No!"

"Ew." But she grinned as she tossed me a tube of toothpaste. "Go rub some of this around in there, will you?"

I used my finger and swished as much as I could at the bathroom sink. I actually felt a lot fresher when I was done. I gave Julia a big, gleaming smile as I handed the toothpaste back.

"Up for a lumberjack?" Julia asked.

We drove to the nearest diner and ordered the lumberjack breakfast again, already falling into a natural habit of splitting up the drinks.

But the lumberjack looked different. It came with a heap of beans.

"Lovely," Julia said. "A steaming pile of—"

"Who wants to eat *beans* for breakfast?" I asked.

"A lumberjack." She looked sideways at Addie, who was happily teething on a rainbow set of plastic baby keys. "Addie, would you like to try some beans?"

"Can she eat beans?"

Julia picked up a bean and mashed it with her fingers. "The middle's soft enough. I'll just squish it out of the skin part."

She placed the middle of a bean in Addie's mouth. Addie gummed it, and her face fell, like she'd never eaten anything so disgusting. She stuck her tongue out and Julia scooped off the yucky bean.

"That's probably for the best. I don't really want you to have to change a bunch of beany diapers in the backseat today."

I laughed and we divvied up the good parts of the breakfast.

Would Mom and Dad feel sad that they missed Addie trying her first bean? Or going for her first swim yesterday?

Julia would probably say *Who cares?*

Would she really mean it?

"So, where are we going today?"

"Up," Julia said.

"Up?"

She threw a brochure on the table. It was for a mountain.

"I've never heard of this mountain."

"We're like eight hours from home."

"We are?"

"Yes, where were *you* yesterday?"

"Sleeping."

"Well, stay awake more today. Get in with Addie. Read to her or something."

I wished that Mom and Dad had gotten me my summer reading books before I'd left, because I could have been reading them. Or a blank notebook I could have started my journal in. Maybe I could have journaled this trip. But instead, they'd gotten me a heap of science books I hadn't even wanted.

15

There had been yelling.

We weren't really the yelling sort of family, but if there was yelling, I didn't like it. So I hid in my room like I always did when that happened. I turned on some music.

There was *a lot* of yelling.

Then, when it stopped, I waited.

While I don't like yelling, I do get curious about things.

So I decided I needed a glass of water, and I tiptoed to the kitchen.

Mom and Dad and Julia were all sitting around the table, but Julia was in Mom's lap, like she was a little, little girl, curled up and cuddling. It was the first, and last, time she ever looked small to me.

Everyone was crying.

I snuck past, afraid to cancel my pretend mission halfway through. I got a glass and turned on the faucet at the sink and filled the glass up, nice and slow.

When I turned, Dad had come around the table and had his arms around Mom and Julia. They were all still crying.

I stood there, frozen and stupid, with my glass of water I didn't even need.

They looked like this *family*. This family that was all complete, just the three of them.

I debated. I debated going over there and hugging Dad from outside all of it. Or sneaking under his arm to be on the inside.

But they looked like they'd forgotten all about me.

Like I didn't exist.

As part of the family, or otherwise.

I headed upstairs, my feet a bit too loud, and I spilled my water.

Nobody helped me clean it up.

I was on my own.

16

"Carter asked me to marry him."

"He what?"

I looked up at the rearview mirror from my seat in the back next to Addie. I lifted her bare toes to her mouth so she could suck on them. She loved doing that and I needed her to be busy. Julia caught my eye in the mirror only for a second.

"You aren't old enough to get married."

Julia laughed. "I *am* old enough to get married. Remember, I turned eighteen? That was the birthday my own kid spit up on me when it was time to blow out the candles?"

I smiled. That had been funny, actually. A lot of people had been there, and Julia was dressed all nice, but she had been holding Addie when someone brought the cake out to her. She had looked so beautiful and somehow graceful and loving as she handed Addie off to Mom and went to get changed. She returned in leggings and a sweatshirt and said *that's better* and took Addie back, and then Carter lit the candles for her again.

"Better than seventeen, when you had morning sickness, you remember that one? You were the one puking then."

"Yeah, that was confusing. We didn't know why yet. My friends were probably so grossed out when I ran to the bathroom at the restaurant. And the staff probably thought I'd been drinking before I got there." She laughed, but I wasn't sure if I wanted to. Yet.

I looked at Addie, who had forgotten her toes and seemed to be getting sleepy again.

"Anyway, *Carter*," I said.

"Right, Carter. He asked me to marry him."

"Yeah. What did you say?"

"No, of course!"

"What do you mean, *of course?*"

"I don't want to marry Carter. Maybe I would have, you know, *before* Addie happened, but since she *did* happen, now, I don't know, it seemed like we *had* to get married, to make something broken fixed."

"Is that why things have been funny between you two?"

"What do you mean?"

"He asked me if you were okay."

"Did he really?"

"Yeah. I think he was worried."

"Well, we can't just break up, either, you know? He's Addie's father. He'll be in the picture *forever*. Even when I'm with someone else."

I unbuckled my seat belt.

"What are you doing?" Julia asked, her eyes flicking to look at me in the mirror again.

"Coming to be with you."

I wiggled my way into the front passenger seat as Julia said, "Please Lord don't let me crash this car right now because my parents will kill me Amen."

She *was* taking us up. Up a mountain, just like she had said. Beyond the metal rail, the ground was getting farther and farther away.

"So how far from home are we now?"

"I don't know."

"Are we heading toward home, or farther from it?"

"I don't know."

"Come on, you must know something."

"Do I look like a GPS? Have you seen me using a GPS?"

"No."

"No." She picked up the brochure and thrust it at me. "I just read the directions from there."

"Oh." There was a little picture map, but it was cartoony and didn't look like a real place. "So . . . if we aren't headed toward home, we won't make it there tonight, because there aren't enough hours left in the day."

"Hm. That's probably true," she said in a sarcastic voice, as if she hadn't considered it.

"Should I call Dad, then, and tell him we got delayed? We need another day?"

"Don't call Dad."

"What about Carter?"

"Don't call Carter either."

"But doesn't Carter need to know where Addie is?"

"No. Addie's with me."

Was she serious?

I sighed.

"What part of *I'm leaving* didn't you understand? I was leaving. As in not coming back."

I shrank down in my seat. Outside the window, the mountains looked taller and taller.

"I think I understood that part. The part I don't get is the *you come too* part."

"I'll admit that's become confusing for me, too." Julia sounded super angry.

"I mean, if you were leaving forever, what was going to happen to me?"

"I don't know. I just . . . I just . . ." Julia stopped talking.

"Um . . . ," I said when she seemed to have settled down. "If you were *leaving* leaving, and Carter doesn't know, did you . . . kidnap Addie?"

Julia nodded slowly.

Then she said, "I also kidnapped you."

17

My big sister was a kidnapper.

She pulled the car over at a "scenic overlook." That's what the sign said. We got out.

There were other cars there. Normal families with married parents and nobody kidnapped.

Julia watched my eyes taking in these families, counting their members, analyzing them, as she hitched Addie tighter on her hip. "You don't know anything about them," she said. "And they don't know anything about you."

"Go see the view." I took Addie. "I'll change her."

We'd developed a decent system for changing her in the backseat, so I did that pretty quickly, and had her back up against my shoulder in a couple minutes.

"What a nice big sister you are," a friendly but obviously evil woman said to me.

But I wasn't the big sister. I was the little sister.

I thought about saying *I'm her auntie, you dolt,* but what

came out instead was "You don't know anything about me and I don't know anything about you!"

She looked startled, like I had punched her, which was so funny I wished Julia had seen it.

"I suppose that's true, love," she said. "I suppose that's true. Is there anything we should know about each other?"

"What brings you to this here mountain?" I asked, making fun of her.

"Anniversary road trip. Our fiftieth!" She beamed.

"Sweet," I said.

"And yourself?"

"I don't think we know yet. Enjoy your trip!"

I hurried away from the woman, as if I had somewhere to go. I looked for Julia along the rock wall that kept people from falling into the view, but when I saw her, I stopped walking.

Without us, she seemed alone, but not lonely.

She looked out at other mountains and between them at the fields and cows and roads and lakes and little houses. Like she could see the whole wide world.

I'd had to help get Julia's room ready. Mostly because she was getting too uncomfortable to move things around like that, and, with Mom and Dad on actual furniture duty, it seemed to be the little sister's job to sort through piles of old clothes and the remains of a childhood about to be thrown in the garbage.

Julia acted like this was the best opportunity for fun we'd had in a long time.

"Maybe you'll want some of my old clothes," she said.

Because we were six years apart, I hadn't grown up wearing her hand-me-downs like most little sisters. Mom hadn't saved a lot of Julia's clothes, except for a few things for sentimental reasons, and then by the time they had me, Julia was old enough to wear her clothes for a long time and then just keep them until they were worn out. Sometimes there was a sweater or something, but not too often.

The plan for the bedroom was to move out Julia's desk and put the crib there; they were going to get rid of her old dresser and get a lower one that could also be a changing table. Most of the drawers would be for Julia's clothes and then one for diapers and clothes for the baby. The baby would, apparently, grow so fast that she didn't need lots of clothes in any one size and everything she needed for a few weeks at a time could fit in a drawer.

So my job was to help Julia cut down on her stuff so she could store it in less space.

I dumped out all the clothes drawers in the middle of the floor. We were sorting into three piles: Julia, Cassie, charity.

"How about this? When was the last time you wore this?" I held up a patterned shirt.

"Um, before I got the beach ball implanted in my stomach." Julia giggled from the bed.

"Will you wear it again after you have the beach ball removed?"

"I have no idea. You pick a pile."

"I'm not going to just pick a pile. What'll happen is, in a

year you'll say I gave away or took all your favorite things. . . . How about this green dress?"

"Green dress, schmeen dress."

"Julia!"

"Sorry!"

"How about this: If you've worn it junior year or later, say 'keep,' okay?"

"Okay, sure."

I held up something.

She shook her head.

Something else.

She shook her head again.

"Jul-i-a!"

"I'm sorry." She wasn't. She giggled.

"At this rate, you will have empty drawers, and you will have to come home from the hospital and raise your baby naked."

"Oh well. Then I'll have to buy new clothes. All-new clothes for an all-new life."

I paused.

"Not everything in your life will be new."

Julia looked at me. For the first time that hour, she was being serious. "But my life will never be the same again."

I wanted to hug her. At least, part of me did. Or maybe ask her to tell me more about it, then tell her everything was going to be okay.

But I didn't want to be the one taking care of her. She was bigger than me. She was supposed to take care of me. And there I was, kneeling hip-deep in a pile of clothes, trying to make her tell me if she would ever wear any of it again because Lord knew she had to wear *something* when she was a mom.

My sister was going to be a mom.

She was watching me. I cleared my throat.

"How about this? How about if I make the three piles, and you can look through, and if you feel one way or the other about something, you can just fix it, okay? Like when we can't decide if we want pizza or Chinese and then I pick one and you see if you feel sad?"

"Yeah, okay," she said.

"Okay?"

"Yeah." She smiled. "I said *okay.*"

I came up beside Julia and put my free arm around her. She kept looking out.

I held Addie tight, away from the edge.

"Hey, Julia?"

"Yeah?"

"Can today be the new best day you've had in a long time?"

"I would like that. I would like that an awful lot."

"Go ahead then. Keep taking us up. I won't call home on you."

18

The mountain turned out to be so beautiful and also a lot cooler than everywhere else had been lately. I was glad I'd brought a sweatshirt. We pulled over at another rest area to put Addie in pajamas because that was really the only long stuff we had for her. I sat in back with her again after that, clapping her hands together and then letting her stick her fingers in my mouth to check out my teeth.

"Does she ever bite you when she eats?" I asked Julia.

"Yeah, sometimes. It hurts!"

"What do you do about it?"

"I ping her."

"You *ping* her? Are you allowed to do that?"

Julia caught my eye in the rearview mirror again.

Right. Are you allowed to feed her beans? To take her on a vacation so her dad doesn't know where she is? What was the point of all these questions?

"Just on her foot. It gets her attention. She has to eat, and she can't eat if she does that."

I nodded.

There were a lot more travelers heading up the mountain.

"What if there's no place to stay?"

"What do you mean?"

"What if there's no place to stay? I mean, no empty rooms?"

"Who are you, the Virgin Mary?"

"Yep. We'll have to swaddle Addie and lay her in a manger."

"Away in a manger, no room at the inn," Julia sang from the front seat. Addie turned to try to figure out where the singing was coming from.

"She likes when you sing," I said.

"I sound terrible when I sing."

"You don't."

Julia used to put me to bed, when I was four and she was ten. I asked for her specifically, every night. She'd sing me the ABCs and then "Twinkle, Twinkle," which were the same tune, so that was perfect. One night she sang me "Itsy-Bitsy Spider" and then I sleepily asked, *Why are you making me think of spiders at bedtime?* and she laughed and I laughed and she said not to worry, it was just a song. And then she would read me a book and I would never hear the end of the book because I would be asleep.

"I've always loved the way you sing."

"I know there's a room, by the way, because I called ahead, when you were trying to clean your teeth this morning. They usually wouldn't have had one so late, but there was a cancellation. So it's ours, just for one night."

"Amazing. . . . Is it a hundred dollars again?"

"Don't you worry about that. You know what, though? It's

a nice-enough place, I bet they'll give you a free toothbrush at the front desk."

The car climbed and climbed the mountain and finally we got to the beautiful, fancy log cabin of a hotel at the top.

"It's more expensive, isn't it?"

"Ask me no questions."

Julia's head was in the clouds as much as this mountain was. But like, literally. I could see them, the little clouds now below the mountain.

Had she really needed this so bad?

I supposed it was worth my life savings. If she had been going to become a crazy person had we all stayed home.

Our room was a little nicer than the one the night before, and high up, with a view of the mountains.

"We were lucky to get this view!" I said.

"It's the top of a mountain," Julia said. "Every room has a view."

I claimed the bed by the glass doors to the porch.

"Shall we check out today's pool?" Julia asked in a snooty voice.

"Certainly, dear sister."

We stopped, of course, for Addie to eat a little.

I regretted forgetting to dry the bikini but wiggled into it anyway. The big T-shirt was a lost cause, so I rummaged around in my duffel bag for a smaller one.

"Don't," Julia said.

"Huh?" I looked up.

"Don't cover it." Julia had a sort-of-crooked smile.

I stared at her.

Then her smile turned real. "Looks good. *You* look good."

"Oh. . . . Thanks."

"Don't forget to sunscreen that white stomach of yours."

I looked down. She was totally right; my stomach was super pale from my wearing competitive suits all the time.

"But not today," she said. "The pool is inside. We'll meet you there when we finish."

I followed the arrows through the hallways to the pool and got in.

It felt like being outside because it was all glassed in with huge windows, and from there you could see the mountains, just like Julia had said. Like swimming in the sky.

Julia showed up with Addie and handed her over with no hesitation—"Dunk her all you like"—and went to sit in the hot tub. Addie and I had a great time.

Later, in our room, Julia asked if I'd brought anything fancy to wear.

"Fancy? Let me explain again that I had no time, and no idea where we were going."

"Hm." Julia bit her lip, thinking.

She dumped all our clothes out onto the beds. When my phone tumbled out, I grabbed it and turned it on, but there were no bars on it way up here on the mountain, so I shut it back off. She gave me a look, but I shrugged. "I promised. I'm not going to call anyone."

Julia dug through our clothes and came up with two black tops she thought were good enough. "Here." She handed me one of them. "And your long jeans." Then she decorated us with lip gloss and eye shadow and mascara.

She paused over Addie, who really only had the jammies. "Oh well," she said. "She's a baby, and it's nighttime."

And then we went down to the fancy restaurant.

It was probably the closest thing to a romantic dinner I'd ever had, except it was with my sister and her kid.

Nobody seemed to mind the baby, or that we were young. Everyone cooed over Addie in her carrier and eventually she dozed off. We ordered entrees and nothing else, but that also seemed to be okay.

While we were sitting there, the sun set, right outside the windows. Well, maybe not *right* outside, but it was beautiful.

Our waitress brought us sparkling water in champagne flutes.

"Cheers." Julia held up her glass, and I clinked mine to it.

After the waitress walked away, I said, "I don't really like bubbles in my water."

"It's just for fun," Julia said. "It's cute."

"Yeah, I guess." I set down my glass. "You didn't really kidnap me, you know. I decided to come."

"I know. Trouble is, when you're twelve, what you want and what you decide doesn't matter as much as what the grown-ups think."

"I've noticed."

Julia laughed. "Of course you have."

Back in our room, we turned off all the lights and went out on the porch to look at the stars. There were more of them than at home, and they were brighter. Really the best darn display the heavens had ever put on.

"I love it here," Julia said.

"Me too," I said.

But a hard lump twisting in the pit of my stomach was making me feel like I should probably spend some time in the bathroom.

Because I had told Dad that we would be home.

And we weren't home at all.

We were far away and happy, at the top of a mountain.

And nobody, nobody else in the world, knew where we were.

19

The sunrise was beautiful, too. We were up with Addie. But we didn't mind. We went back to sleep after that, until ten o'clock. We put everything in the car for checkout and went back to the fancy restaurant for breakfast.

I read the menu a dozen times, looking for it.

"No lumberjack today, Cass."

"I know."

"What should we have instead?"

"French toast. It says it comes with strawberries."

"You do that. I'll get blueberry pancakes."

"Done."

The food was so good.

We piled into the car and just sat.

"Where to?" Julia finally asked.

The question hung in the air. Was she waiting to see if I would ask to go home?

I pushed down the nagging voice of my conscience that

said that Dad must be freaking out and Mom was probably having a nervous breakdown. They knew we were together. They trusted Julia, didn't they?

And didn't they trust me? If I was trying to be a good sister to Julia and make this the fun escape she wanted, wouldn't they want me to do that? To be supportive like they were always saying?

Plus, I was mad at them.

What about what *I* wanted? Would they even care?

I was having a good time out with Julia. I wanted to be with her. I didn't want to be at swimming with Liana and stupid Piper, and I didn't want to be with Mom and Dad.

So what if we were burning through my life savings and what Julia had earned from Grandma for being responsible and struggling to finish high school? So what?

Julia was going to be a mom for the rest of her life and I was going to have to go back to school eventually. So . . . so what?

I was the one who'd told her to go away. I was going to have to be the one to fix this.

"You know what's at the bottom of this mountain?" Julia asked.

"What?"

"Swap our pool swim for a lake today?"

"Perfect."

Mom and Dad had taken us to a lake once, had rented a cabin for a week.

I was ten and Julia was sixteen.

In the mornings, Dad and I would swim or explore the lake in a canoe; Mom would park herself, with books, in one of the Adirondack chairs; Julia would take over the picnic table with her huge SAT prep guides. After a lunch of sandwiches, we'd play board games or go hiking on the trails around the lake, and come back for burgers and hot dogs cooked on the charcoal grill.

It was weird to remember those days without Addie; I built her into the memories in a high chair by the picnic table, or strapped to someone's chest for the hikes.

Like in a way, Addie had always been part of us, even before we knew her.

The lake was clear and smooth.

"Here, take her in." Julia handed me Addie. "Just don't get water in her mouth. You never know if there's bacteria or something."

"Okay."

After our paddle party, we lay out on beach towels on the sand.

"You had towels in the car?" I asked Julia.

She smiled.

Before she could even ask, I wiped Addie's hands and face and luscious toes with baby wipes, re-slathered her in sunscreen, and fed her a jar of carrots.

"I'll keep her," Julia said, "if you want to go back in on your own."

"Sure."

"Stay out in the middle where I can see you. Don't adventure too far."

"Okay."

I did some fast freestyle back and forth in front of the little beach area. It felt good to get my heart going. When I was winded, I stopped and waved to Julia. She waved back. Addie was cuddled against her, probably eating.

I flipped onto my back and spread my arms wide, staring up into the sky.

Dad and I had taken the canoe out.

Most days, we went "adventuring"—my word for exploring all the inlets and secret passages that connected the lake to other lakes.

But that day, arms aching from days of paddling, we just went out to the middle of the water, pulled our paddles in, and floated.

"What perfect clouds," Dad said.

I tipped my head way back, so I could see them from under the visor of my baseball cap.

They were, like in a movie.

White. And puffy, puffy.

"What do you see?" he asked.

"A turtle."

"Ah, yeah, me too. What about that over there? It looks like a big bird."

"Maybe it's the international swimming symbol. The wave with the person doing freestyle, side view."

"And look, two girls."

"I don't see two girls."

"Right over there."

"Do you know they're girls because they have pigtails and skirts?"

"No. They don't have pigtails or skirts."

"Oh. Well, I don't see them. I see . . . I see . . ."

As I waited for it to come to me, the last of the fluffy clouds drifted by and before long there was nothing at all but blue.

"What do you see now?" Dad asked.

"The sky."

"Try harder."

I leaned back farther. "This lake. Reflected."

"Ooo! That's better."

"Infinity."

"Wow. That's true, too."

"The sky goes on and on forever."

"Especially since you already said it was like a mirror," Dad said.

"What do you see?"

"I still see two girls."

"You do?"

"Yeah. They're everywhere."

"Dad—"

"Center of my world. And my infinity."

I looked back down into the boat, at our water bottles and my rubber river shoes. "What about Mom?"

"Well, that goes without saying. I wouldn't have them without her. . . . You hungry?"

"Always."

"Let's head back. I think I can get there on my own." Dad, from the back of the canoe, picked up his paddle and alternated his strokes, aiming us back toward Mom and Julia.

20

"You've been quiet," Julia said, glancing at me in the rearview mirror.

I shrugged.

"You okay?"

"Sure."

"Thinking too much?"

"Maybe." I wiggled the plastic keys in front of Addie. She reached for them. I lifted them higher, and she reached higher. Then I hid them behind her car seat. She turned to look. "Smarty-pants." I dropped the keys in her lap. She picked them up and gummed them. "Where are we sleeping tonight?"

"Probably somewhere out along the highway. I think we won't get lucky again out here where it's resorty."

I really wanted to take a shower after swimming in the lake. I felt sandy and sticky and somehow green.

"So . . . we're not going home?"

"Do you want to?"

I looked out the window some more.

When Addie fell asleep, I climbed up to the front seat with Julia.

"What?" she asked as I buckled.

"What are we going to say to them?"

"Who?"

"You know who. Mom and Dad."

"Oh, Mom and Dad."

"They must be going crazy."

Julia pressed her lips together tight.

"Couldn't we call and make some kind of deal, like we can travel as long as we want if we call them every night?"

"That's like asking permission. I don't want to ask permission."

I nodded. "*I* could ask permission. Like, for me. You don't have to talk to them. Maybe if I did it would be enough, and at least they won't call the police or whatever. Maybe we could have longer."

After five minutes, Julia said, "Plug your phone in."

I found my phone in my bag and plugged it in. My hands were shaking. What was I going to say to them? How much trouble would we be in?

I turned the phone on.

We sat in silence as a hundred texts pinged in.

"Mom or Dad?" Julia asked.

"Mmm . . . Dad. Mom might cry or yell or something."

"Good choice. It's always been easier to make a deal with Dad. . . . Once when I was really little, I made a deal with him that I could have a scoop of ice cream for every piece of broccoli I ate."

"Did he give it to you?"

"Oh yeah. I fell asleep in the world's biggest bowl of ice cream. He totally won, though. I was so full of broccoli, I hardly ate any of it."

I pictured her at the table, little, snoozing in a bowl of ice cream. There had been a time when our family *was* just Mom and Dad and Julia.

In her memory, did it *feel* like I was there, the way I sometimes felt like Addie had been there before?

Julia pulled off the side of the road at a gas station with some picnic tables. "Go."

I unplugged the phone, hoping the little charge would be enough, and went over to sit at an empty picnic table.

He picked up, first ring.

"Cassie?"

"Hi, Daddy."

"Don't you *Hi-Daddy* me."

He was right. I never called him Daddy.

"Where the hell are you?"

"Um . . ." I peered toward the road, to see if there were any signs. "A gas station. Just making a pit stop. You know."

"Are you all okay?"

"Yes, Dad, of course we are."

"Are you headed home?"

"Not yet. We need more time."

"Time to do what?"

"I don't know."

"You *don't know*? How can it be so important if you don't know?"

There are plenty of things that are important that you don't know.

Dad took in a breath and let it out like he was trying to be calm and patient, to think before he spoke. "Cassie, just come home, we can sort it out—"

"You aren't listening to me! You never listen to me!"

Dad was silent. Maybe because he was mad at me for yelling, or maybe because he was trying to show he was going to listen.

"Can we make a deal?" I asked.

"A deal?"

"Yeah. You let us have our vacation, and I'll call you every night to say we're okay."

He thought. Then he said, "You will call in the morning and at night. You will text the name and address of the place you're staying. You will send a photo of the three of you every day."

I thought. "Okay."

"If you don't, I'm coming to get you."

"How can you? You don't know where I am."

"We're tracking your phones."

My stomach went swoopy again.

"So why did you ask where we are?"

"I was giving you a chance to tell me."

My eyes stung.

But what was the point of telling them things if they didn't listen?

"Dad? How's Mom?"

"She's upset. . . . She wants to know why."

I nodded. Not that he could see.

"Do you need money?" Dad asked. "Because we don't really—"

"No. This is our thing. We're paying for it."

"Can I talk to Julia?"

I glanced over at the car. Julia was pretending not to watch. Probably because she saw me rubbing at my eyes. "No. She doesn't want to."

"I need to hear her voice or the deal is off. I need to know she's okay. And Addie."

"Addie's sleeping."

"Julia then. And a picture of Addie."

"Yeah, yeah, okay."

I walked back over to the car. Julia leaned to peer through my window. I held out the phone.

"You don't have to take it," I said. "Just say something."

"Pickles," she said.

I put the phone back to my ear. "Okay?"

"Okay. And the picture. And you'll call tonight."

"Yeah. Bye, Dad."

Before I climbed in the car, I took a pic of Addie sleeping and sent it.

I got in the car, took a deep breath.

"Hey." Julia rubbed my back. "Thanks, Cass. I mean it.

You're ten times braver than I am. . . . Though I did text Carter while you were gone." Her phone was plugged in, turned off again but charging. "Said we were away, not to worry." When I was breathing normally, she asked, "Terms?"

"Calls morning and night. The hotel address. A picture of all of us every day."

"You do the calls. I'll do the rest. Time limit?"

I shook my head. "I just said we needed some."

"Perfect, perfect, perfect."

I looked over at her.

She was smiling.

My body relaxed.

She started the car.

Eventually the mountains fell away. The land looked a little flatter. Still hilly, just not as steep or tall. The trees were more spread out. Lot of farms. Some horses and cows. A few churches. Ranch houses set far apart.

I was sitting with my feet up on the dashboard, absent-mindedly playing with the anklet from Liana, when it broke.

"Crap." I held up the broken strands.

"What is that?" Julia asked, glancing over.

"Friendship anklet. Well, sort of. I mean, it was. I mean . . ."

"That isn't real, right?"

My heart stopped. "What?" I looked out my window, but I couldn't see anything scary.

"A drive-in movie. Like from the old days. Like you pull

your car up to the speakers." Julia took the exit and drove along to the hill where they had the movies. "Just five dollars a car," she read off the sign. "And it's a double feature!"

Julia drove up to the ticket booth.

The older man inside looked at his watch, then at the clock on the wall of his booth, and sighed. "You're three hours early."

"That's okay," Julia said. "We just wanted the best seat in the house."

The big, wide world of a house.

We couldn't stop giggling.

"Is concessions open?" Julia asked.

"Over there." The man pointed to a little house nearby. "I'll tell them to turn on the popcorn machine."

"Thanks."

Julia parked in a front-row spot and walked over to concessions. She came back with a huge bucket of popcorn.

We sat in the front seat with our feet on the dashboard, hands meeting again and again in the slippery popcorn bucket between us.

"Why haven't you been hanging out with Liana and Piper?" Julia asked.

"Why won't you go out with Maya and Remy?"

"Quit getting popcorn everywhere," Julia said as I dropped half of my fistful.

"*You're* getting popcorn everywhere." I threw the rest in my hand at her.

"Hey!" She whipped a handful back at me. "You're making—a mess—of my car!"

When I grabbed the bucket, she was out the driver's-side

door in a flash. I jumped out on my side and ran around, throwing a huge scoop at her. She shrieked, but instead of running for it, she lunged for the bucket. Some of the popcorn spilled, but she managed to get a handful anyway.

"Julia! EW!"

She'd rubbed popcorn in my hair.

I moved away, and as I spun to run for it, I threw the rest of the popcorn in her direction. It got all over her. The bucket hit the ground, and then we both leaned against the car, laughing and panting.

"Don't say you're hungry later." Julia picked up the popcorn bucket, peering inside to see how much was left.

"You know what I am? So thirsty."

"Stay here," she said.

Where else would I go?

She headed back to concessions and returned with two huge sodas, each in a bucket almost as big as the one for popcorn.

"Coke." She handed one to me.

I slurped it so fast I sneezed.

We climbed back into the car.

I was so thirsty I kept guzzling that soda, all the way down to the bottom of the bucket.

Other cars pulled up and it got dark out.

Addie woke up crying. Julia changed her in the back and brought her around to the front seat to feed her. "The movie should start soon."

And it did. The screen lit up. People sitting on the hoods of their cars clapped.

But I jumped out of my seat and out of the car.

"Where are you going?" Julia called through the window.

"I have to pee!" I shouted back, running toward concessions, hoping there was a bathroom there.

Julia was laughing at me.

When I got back in the car, she said, "Okay?"

"Yep."

"You couldn't have gone like, *before* the movie started? We were sitting here for hours."

"You sabotaged me with the world's biggest soda."

"I know." Julia laughed again. "I almost wish I'd done it on purpose."

"Yeah, yeah." I scooched over and rested my head on her shoulder.

Julia jostled me awake. "Put your seat belt on. Make your phone call. Use the house line."

They were less likely to answer. And they didn't. Maybe on purpose.

So I left a voice mail. Just saying we were all still fine.

Julia drove us to a motel that was okay, not nice like that mountain lodge palace in the sky, but okay, because Addie was there in her little Pack 'n Play and Julia didn't even bother to go to a different bed, she just curled up in mine with me.

21

When I woke up, I realized my hair had dried in clumps. I itched. "I want to take a shower."

"You? A shower?" Julia hit me with a pillow.

"I'm covered with lake and salt and butter and popcorn."

"If I had known a popcorn bombardment was going to be the trick to getting you to shower, I would have tried it years ago."

"Shut up. Swimming in chlorine every day is like taking a shower."

"Sure."

"Can I borrow your hairbrush?"

She went over to our bags and dug around. She tossed me the hairbrush.

"Thanks."

When we climbed into the car, I said, "Your car stinks like a movie theater."

"Thanks. You can scrounge around and eat whatever popcorn you can find for breakfast."

"Julia!"

"Just kidding, we'll stop. But please feel free to eat the popcorn you got everywhere."

"Will do."

Our morning diner had our favorite breakfast.

When we spotted it on the menu, we gave a brief chant of "Lum-ber-jack, lum-ber-jack."

"People are looking at us," I whispered.

Julia stifled a giggle behind her hand as the waitress came over. Julia said, sweetly, "We'll have the lumberjack, please."

I wolfed down my share of the eggs and toast, and tried to steal more bacon, but Julia knocked my hand out of the way with a jab of her fork and got the last piece.

She polished off the bacon and stirred more sugar into her coffee. "Any particular kind of place you'd like to go?"

"Everything we do is great."

"Maybe we shouldn't drive so far today. Maybe we should find a hotel with a pool again, and just . . . hang out. Would that be okay?"

"Yeah. Are you tired?"

"Yeah, a little."

"That's fine then."

I called Dad while we drove, on the house phone again. Again, no one answered. I said we were all good and hung up.

We didn't drive too far, but we did go off the highway, to a bed-and-breakfast. The open room had only one bed, which was fine for us because we'd been sharing anyway. The room was flowery and overdecorated.

"The floor looks okay in here." Julia examined the plush carpet and spread out a baby blanket. "Better than a hotel anyway. Let Addie roll around a bit; she's been spending too much time in that car seat."

I put Addie on the blanket and lay down next to her, teasing her with toys to make her roll over.

"Sorry to disappoint," Julia said, "but you know they won't have the lumberjack tomorrow? Bed-and-breakfasts serve you something fancy that they pick out."

"What if you don't like it? What if you're allergic?"

"I'm sure they make accommodations. Also"—she sighed— "we may have to eat with *other people*."

"*Other people?*" I wrinkled my nose.

"I don't like it, either." Julia dropped onto the squishy bed and clicked the TV remote, flipping through the channels.

Addie rolled over again.

"She's pretty easy, this baby." I crawled over to the diaper bag and got a diaper and wipes.

"You're getting good at taking care of her. You're doing stuff before I even think to."

"You know? You're pretty cool for a mom."

"What do you mean?"

"I mean you just let me take care of her like you aren't worried about it."

"I'm not worried about it."

"Not at all?"

"No. I'm taking a nap now. You can go out if you want. There's a stroller for her in the car; you could take her down one of the paths. I want to go swimming later, though, okay?"

"Yeah, okay."

I got Addie dressed again—no longer in mountain-ville, she was back in her normal cutesy summer clothes—and even remembered to put sunscreen on her cheeks, and I took her out for a walk, just the two of us.

"Look, Addie, there's a bunny." I came around the front of the stroller and pointed.

She looked in the direction of the bunny and tried to sit up.

The bunny ran away and Addie looked into my face instead.

"What do you think about all day?" I asked her.

"Mah mah. Gooby bleh."

"Yeah, me too."

I went back to pushing the stroller, admiring Addie's little bare feet sticking out in front of us, pointing the way.

The bed-and-breakfast's pool didn't have chlorine, but something else, maybe salt or bromine. It was built to look like a pond, sloping in naturally, like a beach but with sand only for your eyes and not for your feet. There were even some "rocks" jutting out to swim around.

"I think we should call this our grand tour of places to swim," I said to Julia.

I waded in. The pool wasn't good for laps. My body kind

of missed them. If I ever did end up back home on the team, would I even be able to win races?

Would there be anyone cheering for me?

Or would my friends be glad if I lost?

"What's on your mind?" Julia asked, joining me in the water with Addie in her arms.

I shrugged.

"You're missing something."

I looked at her carefully.

Oh, Julia, weren't we always missing something?

Even at home, I hadn't felt whole. Not for a long time.

Run away, I was so happy, but . . . what on earth were Mom and Dad feeling? A few days ago, they'd had a house full of girls, of noise and laughing and arguing, too. And suddenly, nobody at all.

If Julia had left by herself, and never said anything to me, never said goodbye, how would I have felt?

Exactly like Mom and Dad were feeling, probably.

My stomach squirmed. I pulled my arms around me, still standing only thigh-deep in the water.

"Cass?" Julia looked at me, real searching and gentle. "You don't . . . *want* to go home now, do you?"

I shook my head. Started to shiver, standing half in, half out of the water.

I reached for Addie. Julia handed her to me and got out.

I dunked Addie a bit and then we started playing a game.

I would hold her still. Say "Take your mark. . . . *BOOP!*" And rush her through the water. She would shriek and giggle.

When I would hold her still again and say "Take your mark," she would smile so, so big. Not that she understood the words, just that the words meant the fun swooshing part was coming.

Eventually, Julia waded back out to us and watched.

"You're forgetting the 'get set.'"

"There's no 'get set' in swimming. Step up; take your marks; go!" I swooshed Addie again. "You should know that. You've seen enough meets. . . . Maybe it's just been so long since you've been to one."

I stopped, hearing the edge in my voice, and how it must sound to Julia.

She probably hadn't been to a meet in over a year.

I looked at her.

Smile gone. Jaw set.

"Let me take her," Julia said. "She needs—"

"What, a bath? She doesn't need anything!"

Addie was looking between us like *Why are you mad?* and then up at me like *What happened to our game?*

"You know I wasn't going to be able to go to all your swim meets forever anyway."

I started to swoosh Addie gently again, but without the fanfare. Then I handed her back.

Julia sighed, settling Addie on her hip. "You know what would be nice, Cass?"

"What?"

"Another best day ever."

I nodded and walked a couple more inches into the water. "If you have a best day ever, every day, do they still feel as good?"

"Yes. Yes, they definitely do. Perfect days, all in a row, always feel perfect."

But the things to say were building up. Building up in heaps.

And suddenly I wanted her to know all my secrets. Every stupid, mean thing I had ever done or ever even thought.

But I was frozen.

A lake of uncrackable ice.

"Get going, silly," Julia said as she got out of the water. "When you're done, I want to hear the rating on today's swim experience."

Today's swim experience?

Excellent.

Smooth, salty water.

One happy baby.

One favorite sister.

And one big blue sky, stretched out above us, without a single worry.

22

First Julia's T-shirts had just become tight around the middle, like she'd gotten a little belly from eating pizza and not exercising. Julia had always been thin, so that was weird, but not like a stranger would see her and think there was a baby in there.

And then suddenly, it was as if her tummy just popped out, and it *did* look that way. Like there *was* a baby growing in there.

Last summer she did a lot of napping. Mom got her out to the pool sometimes, for exercise, and she went until she felt too embarrassed to go anymore. Most afternoons when I came in from swim practice, she was curled up on the couch, using both a blanket and the air-conditioning. Sometimes she even had her thumb in her mouth. She hadn't been a thumb-sucker.

Mostly, I ignored her, rushing through to a pizza box in the kitchen, to the freezer and the ice cream.

But one day I sat on the floor in front of her, and before long I felt her fingers weaving their way through my hair. I had almost forgotten her touch. I leaned back, relaxed.

"I can feel the baby move," she said.

"Oh," I said.

"Do you want to?"

"How would *I* feel it?"

"Just here, put your hands on my stomach."

I turned around and put my hand on her stomach. "I don't really feel anything."

Julia looked disappointed. "Oh. Do you think I imagined it?"

"I don't think you're imagining anything." But I said it mean.

It wasn't just about the baby kicking that I said it.

Julia was looking down at her bump. She wouldn't meet my eyes.

A lump formed in my throat because of how mean I'd been.

I didn't take it back, but I moved to sit with her on the couch, settling in behind her bent legs, and leaving my hand on her stomach, where she had told me to feel the baby.

My sister had a human being growing inside her.

Maybe it was a lonely thing to feel when you were still a kid yourself.

Maybe she was afraid.

"Cass?"

"Yeah?"

"I have an appointment next week, to see pictures of the baby. You'll come with me?"

"You want me to?"

"Yeah."

"Is it during practice?"

"No, it's in the morning."

So I went. I went with Julia while they took pictures of the alien in her stomach. Mom was there, too, of course, so the tiny room was cramped. I didn't like how many machines there were.

"You said you don't want to know the gender, right?" the technician asked.

"Right," Julia said.

"Look away from the screen for a minute."

Mom looked at the boring cabinets over Julia's head. But Julia looked at me. I understood. If we held our eyes locked on each other, neither of us could cheat. She looked at me and looked at me while a stranger pushed on her belly with a camera trying to figure out the sex of her baby.

"I got what I needed; you can look back at the screen again," the woman said.

Julia's eyes left mine, and when they fixed back on the screen, which was showing the baby's face again, Julia looked so peaceful and happy, like maybe it was a miracle after all that a little person was growing in there, and that, one day, we would get to meet him or her.

23

We ordered pizza to come to the bed-and-breakfast.

We put the box right in the middle of the bed and ate piece after piece.

Best idea ever.

"How can you eat *four* pieces of pizza?" Julia asked.

"You force me to play outside in the water all day and you haven't been feeding me lunch."

"I guess that isn't that different from what you do at home, is it?"

"No, not really. Though usually we do have lunch."

"And you regularly eat half a pizza anyway?"

"Yep. . . . How's our money?"

"Super, actually. Keep eating." She scooped up Addie to feed her. Addie cried a little bit, took longer than usual to get settled.

It didn't bother me.

The pillows were so fluffy. I leaned back with my pizza crust.

Julia's laughing woke me up.

"What, are you just going to sleep in that pizza box?" She pried the crust out of my hand while I tried to mumble an answer. She brushed the hair off my forehead and planted a kiss there.

When she came back from the bathroom, she cuddled me and drowned us in the down covers.

Addie was crying.

I kicked Julia.

"Give her ten minutes."

But she didn't stop.

I kicked Julia again.

She went over to the Pack 'n Play. "Hey, Addie-girl. What's the matter? Hungry?"

She picked her up. Addie stopped crying for only a second.

"Hey, hey. . . ." Julia bounced her for a minute, then paused. Unzipped Addie's pajamas. "Oh no. Cass?"

"Mm?"

Julia turned on the light, brought Addie over. Addie looked all red from crying. She looked from me to her mom, wanting somebody to help her. She wailed.

"Does she feel too hot to you?" Julia asked.

I put the back of my hand on Addie's forehead, my palm on her chest.

I nodded.

Julia left Addie on the bed and got her phone.

"Are you calling Mom and Dad?"

She gave me the evil eye.

"911?" Was Addie *really* sick?

Julia seemed to be reading something on the phone. Then she searched something else.

Addie cried and cried.

"It's okay," I said. "It's okay." But my hands were shaking as I wiggled her the rest of the way out of her pajamas.

Julia got up, pulled on a sweatshirt, put her phone in the pocket, stepped into her flip-flops. Grabbed her keys and wallet.

"Stay with her, okay?"

And she was out the door.

I looked at Addie, lying in the middle of the big bed, still crying.

My heart started pounding.

I thought. Then I went to the bathroom and ran a washcloth under cold water. I squeezed it out and went back to the bed.

"Here . . . here." I folded the washcloth into a rectangle and set it on Addie's forehead. Like they did in movies when someone had a fever. Her crying came down a notch, probably because she was curious about the little towel on her head. After a minute, I moved the washcloth to her chest, and left it there while I got a new diaper and changed her.

"Ah-ih . . . ah-ih . . ." Her sobs turned into hiccups. The hiccups became a clock, marking the passing time. Then she looked around again, probably for Julia, and her lip started quivering, and then she was howling again, this time with hiccups thrown in.

I took off the washcloth.

"Shh . . . shh . . ."

I didn't want to pick her up and make her hotter.

Finally the door burst open. Julia ran over and tossed a drugstore bag on the bed.

She looked at Addie. Relief swept across her face.

"Cass, you about gave me a heart attack! Why are *you* crying?"

"I'm just . . . glad you're back, is all."

Julia made a face at me like I had slapped her. She bit her lip and started opening the boxes she'd got.

An ear thermometer, like we had at home. Julia got it set up and took Addie's temperature.

"Okay. It's one hundred flat. That's not too bad."

Julia took out medicine and an eyedropper. She read the medicine box carefully before she opened the bottle and measured the right amount in the eyedropper.

"Sit her up for me."

I sat Addie up and kept my hand behind her back.

"Thank God there was a twenty-four-hour pharmacy nearby. I was worried there wouldn't be."

Julia started to give her the medicine. Addie made a face and drooled the medicine back out. Julia wiped her shiny lip with the washcloth.

"I need to know you're swallowing this." She gave her the rest of the medicine in one quick squirt, and held Addie's mouth closed until she had swallowed. "There, see it's okay.

It's okay." Julia pulled Addie to her, and then rested against the headboard. She relaxed and eventually Addie relaxed. Stopped crying. Fell asleep.

I sat on the bed, watching.

Finally Julia caught my eye.

"Call Mom and Dad?" she said. "Cass, I got this."

I nodded.

"What did you get all upset about? Did you think I wasn't coming back?"

I swallowed hard.

"Why would you even think that?"

I glared at her.

"Oh. Yeah, I see." She looked down. "I would never leave Addie. And I would never leave you. Not really. I also wouldn't leave you with something you couldn't handle. You did fine. Addie's fine."

I let out the breath I'd been holding. I wanted to cry more. More and more and more.

Julia returned the now-sleeping Addie to the Pack 'n Play.

She came back to our bed. "Aw, Cassie-girl." She cuddled me. "You have to trust me."

"Why should I?"

She stiffened. Her breathing sounded deep and halting, like she was trying not to cry, too.

She hugged me tighter.

After a few minutes, I said, "Who's going to turn off the light?"

And Julia laughed.

24

In the morning, I woke up to see Julia sitting at the end of the bed so she could look into the Pack 'n Play.

"She okay?" I asked.

"Yeah." Julia stood and picked up Addie. Addie was awake, too.

Julia set her on me. Addie cooed softly. Like any other morning. I nestled her into the crook of my arm so she could relax.

"She's cool," I said.

"Yeah," Julia said. "I took her temperature. It's normal."

"Do we have to go to the doctor?"

"The fever was low, so no. So low, it could just be a little bug or even from her teeth. If it gets higher or comes back and sticks around, then we'll go."

"Okay."

"We have to be at breakfast at nine. You want to get her dressed while I take a shower?" She handed me a diaper and a clean outfit of a onesie and little blue shorts.

"Sure."

No lumberjack for us, like Julia had said. But the breakfast was good, some sort of eggy-blueberry French toast thing baked in the oven. And there *were* other people there. About twelve of us at the table.

Everyone was talking, asking each other about their trips.

"And what about you? Are your parents sleeping in?"

"No, we're on our own," Julia said. She had Addie sitting in her lap, facing the table, where she'd scattered a handful of Cheerios. Addie was concentrating on picking them up, but only half of them were making it into her mouth.

"That's interesting. What sparked the trip?" one of the women asked.

"Sisterly bonding time," Julia said. Not the whole story, but enough.

"Isn't that the sweetest thing?" the woman said.

"How old is your baby?" asked another.

"Six months."

"She's adorable."

"Thank you," Julia said.

Not enough people told her Addie was cute. They all spent so much time looking at Julia, trying to figure out how old *she* was. Like her age got in the way of all the normal, polite things people said to each other.

After we escaped from breakfast and went back to our room, Julia said, "We aren't packing today. I've booked us another night."

"Really?"

"Yeah. Figured we could use a rest day after that bad night. The bed was nice though, wasn't it?"

"Yeah. It felt like floating."

"Except, you were sleeping."

"Except, yeah, I was sleeping. And . . ." I'd woken a few more times. Each time, I'd gasped, and then found that it was okay, that Julia was still there next to me, just like she'd been the last time I'd fallen asleep.

"And what?"

"I think I was looking for you."

Her eyebrows went up. "I was right there."

"I . . . I know. So, what are we doing today?"

She tossed me another brochure. "How 'bout a hike? There's a waterfall. We'll put Addie in the chest carrier; we can take turns."

"Yeah, okay."

Julia drove us to the start of the trail and we hiked out to the waterfall. She brought bottles of water and packets of crackers for us, a jar of plums for Addie.

When we got to the waterfall, I was the one wearing Addie on my chest, facing out so she could see.

"Here, turn around." Julia held up her phone. "Smile."

She took our picture. We were always taking pictures of Addie at home. But we'd been keeping our phones off so much, we hadn't really been taking them, except for the one-a-day.

Julia stood next to us and snapped a selfie of the three of us. She tapped around a bit. Sent it to Dad.

He didn't reply.

"Think he's mad?" I asked. "He's been giving us the silent treatment. He asked me to call, but he's not picking up. No one is."

"Maybe he's just giving us the space you asked for." Julia turned her phone back off.

You did have to be quiet to listen.

But if you never said anything back, how did the other person know you'd heard them?

25

It was a Saturday—December 17—when Addie came.

I had been looking forward to Saturday all week. Not because of Addie, of course. We didn't know she was coming that day. Because we were finally going to decorate for Christmas.

Despite the fact that my family had gone all funny, I was excited about Christmas. I'd written a wish list full of stupid things. A sheet of paper front and back. I'd gone to the mall and noted everything that looked mildly appealing. I mean, I deserved all those things, didn't I? I'd been good. I'd been staying out of the way and not doing anything bad.

We hadn't gotten the tree up until late. Julia had stopped going to school after Thanksgiving, having become too fat and uncomfortable, and Mom was taking her to the doctor like every week. Nobody bothered to go to the tree lot.

Finally, on a cold weeknight, I asked Dad, "Aren't we celebrating Christmas? Can't we get a tree?"

"Of course! Of course we're celebrating Christmas." He

looked across the table to Mom. "We'll go pick something out tonight?"

"You two go," she said. "I'll stay here with Julia."

Julia rolled her eyes.

"Did you want to go, honey?" Mom asked.

Julia thought about it. "Not really. It's freezing out and I can't zip my coat."

She could snap it shut at the top, and then it hung wide and open toward the bottom. The argument over whether to buy her a maternity coat for the few weeks she would need one had been loud. She'd said no to almost any suggestion of maternity clothes all fall. She'd only put up with some very plain shirts Mom had bought without her and just put in her room. Otherwise, she'd been in big sweatshirts and sweatpants. Some of them were probably Carter's. Her wearing his clothes, even more than having his baby in her stomach, made him feel omnipresent. He was around a lot anyway, worrying and trying to take care of her when we could do that for her just fine.

"Okay, sport, just you and me," Dad said to me.

There was no one else out shopping for trees that night. I guess most people did that as a family, on the weekend. The way we always had before.

So we got the tree, and the next night Dad put it up, and then for a few days no one even bothered to get out the decorations. I had to beg again, on Friday night, because I was worried we'd get all the way to Christmas with a naked tree. Mom and Dad finally got the boxes from the attic. I untangled the lights, and Dad strung them on the tree.

Julia sat through all of this. She was tired, she said.

Mom dumped a basket of pastel clothes in front of her.

Julia stared at it.

"You wash the clothes ahead," Mom said. "So they're ready. You can fold them while you sit."

Mom left to do more laundry, and Dad had disappeared, too, so it was just me and Julia.

She picked up the tiny feety pajamas, some with little pink pictures on them and some with blue, but a lot with yellow or green or purple. Every once in a while, she would pause, holding up a little onesie.

"Those are so small," I said from my tangle of garlands on the floor.

"They better be small," she said. "The thing still has to come out of me."

We stared at each other for a minute. Then she looked away, and went back to folding.

My stomach knotted.

I got up. "I'm putting on Christmas music."

But in the morning, Julia seemed somehow happy, and busy. Mom and Dad were still in bed, but I was up, opening all the bins of ornaments and sorting through them. Julia was helping me, even though it was hard for her to bend over. She kept wincing and putting her hand on her back.

"Look at you, when you were a little dope." She handed me a laminated-construction-paper ornament I'd made in kindergarten. They'd given us a copy of our school picture, so I'd glued mine in the middle of a star and circled the whole thing in about a pound of glue and glitter. In the picture, I was grinning with no front teeth and my hair was all messy because I couldn't keep it nice between Mom fixing it in the morning and me getting my picture taken after recess.

"I believe this one is yours." I tossed a 3-D geometric construction at her.

"But that's not embarrassing. I made that last year in math class."

Hm. I dug through the boxes. There was nothing embarrassing to Julia.

She used the cardboard top of one of the boxes to make a tray full of sparkly glass ornaments and carried it over to the tree. She had only reached to put the first one on when she asked me to take the tray from her. The tone in her voice made me hurry. She put her hand on her back again.

"You okay?"

"I want to sit down."

I helped her to the couch. I stood there for about five minutes, and then she said, sounding out of breath, "Can you get Mom?"

I ran.

Mom and Dad seemed nervous but cheerful—pretending to be calm?—and then there was a lot of activity: Mom sitting with Julia on the couch but timing something on an app on her phone, Dad making coffee, Mom getting up to check that Julia's bag was all packed the way they'd planned and putting it by the front door.

By the door. Julia's hospital bag. I stared at it.

"Sit with her a few minutes," Mom said to me.

I did.

"Hold my hand?" Julia asked.

I did, but I was afraid to. She squeezed mine suddenly, for like a whole minute, and then she eased up.

"Thanks," she said.

"No problem. Should we, um, tell Carter?"

"We will," Mom said, sweeping back into the room. "When we're sure it's time."

Dad showed up from the kitchen with a plate of orange smiles. He handed it to Julia. "They won't let you eat, love, once you get there, so try to have something now."

We used to sit outside in the summer and eat those orange smiles on the porch. I remember being really little; it could even have been my earliest memory, because Julia had me in her lap and my feet stuck straight out in front, so we might have been like two and eight. We would put the slices in our mouths way up to the rinds, and smile these big orange smiles at each other and laugh and laugh.

And suddenly I pictured another baby who was not me sitting in her lap, eating oranges and giggling and smiling up into Julia's beautiful, happy face, and Julia wasn't a little girl anymore, but grown up.

Mom and Dad were out of the room again.

"Julia?"

"Yeah?"

"You're going to do great," I said.

Then it seemed like two minutes but it was two more hours

and the three of them—four of them, if you included Addie still inside my sister—were out the door on the way to the hospital.

I was by myself, staring at the mess of the living room that I'd wanted to turn into Christmas, bubble wrap and tissue paper strewn all around.

The house felt so quiet and empty.

I thought first to call Grandma. She lived far away, but she'd probably want to know that the baby was coming. Had Mom and Dad already called her? Or did they not want to worry her? Julia could still get sent home, they'd said, but maybe the hospital would keep her, just because she was young.

But I didn't need anyone to talk to. I was fine by myself. Fine.

I kicked one of the ornament boxes.

I would have Christmas, even if my family had left. I would show them.

I started with the ornaments Julia had picked out, in the little cardboard tray. And I thought of her as I hung each one.

Please, let her be okay. Please.

And I put up all our stupid homemade ones from when we were little. And not so little.

I set out Mom's favorite candles on the red runner on the side table. I put the Advent wreath—which had missed most of Advent, for the first time ever—on the dining room table. I couldn't reach to put the star on the tree and the last thing we needed was me in the hospital, too, from falling off a ladder, so I decided that would have to wait. I turned my Christmas music up loud. I wondered if it would be okay for me to make cookies, and decided it would. I followed a recipe in Mom's floury book, and got more flour all over me and the floor, but who cared?

And then when I cut out the gingerbread men with their little-boy shapes, I thought about how waiting for Christmas was all about waiting for a baby.

Dad called, a bunch of times.

"How's Julia?" I asked, again and again.

"Everything's going fine," he would say.

But that didn't answer my question, not exactly. I wanted to know how she *was*. Things going fine didn't mean she wasn't hurting or scared.

"Everything fine at home?"

"Oh yeah, everything's fine." I'd burnt some of the cookies, but not all of them. I was trying to figure out how to make frosting with color dyes. The tips of my fingers were stained rainbow.

"Maya's going to come be with you later."

"Dad, I don't need a sitter."

"Yeah, I know, sport. Call if you want, okay?"

"Sure, Dad."

He called me back when it had been dark out for hours and hours.

His voice sounded different. Worn out but entirely happy.

"You're an auntie!" he said.

And Julia felt a million miles away.

Because she was a mom now.

"What is it?"

"A girl! Adele Cassandra."

My eyes filled up.

Why would Julia put my name in the baby's name?

"They're doing great. Don't worry, okay? Mom's with her. She and I are going to stay here tonight, so Maya's going to come spend the night with you. Tomorrow, you can come meet your niece, okay?"

26

We finished our day in the B and B pool.

"No pizza," Julia said when we talked about dinner.

"What, then?"

"Let's go to the little town, maybe we'll see something we like."

So we got back in the car again.

We found an Italian place. "I guess you can get pizza," Julia said. "But I'm going to order some spinach or salad for the table. Actually, how 'bout an artichoke?"

"Yeah, okay."

She ordered pasta and I ordered a personal pizza. Julia gave Addie a short piece of plain noodle to gum.

"Was today the best day you had in a long time?" I asked.

"You know, I've been having a lot of good ones recently. Tomorrow, no pizza."

"Yes, Mom."

"Arrooo!" Addie shrieked.

"What are you, a werewolf now? Werebaby?"

"How many good days has it been?"

"I think maybe six."

I tried to count it. "Lumberjack. Lumberjack with beans. No lumberjack. Lumberjack. No Lumberjack. Five days."

She threw a chunk of bread stick at my forehead.

"Trust you to count it by food."

"How would you have counted it?"

"I might have counted it—and I would have expected you to count it—by stops on the great swim tour."

"Oh, you mean like this: hotel pool, mountain lodge pool, shining lake, pretend-natural pool, pretend-natural pool?"

"Yes, something more like that."

"Arrooo!" Addie shrieked again.

"Toss your werebaby another noodle."

Julia pinched off another piece. "What do you think she'll be like when she's older?"

"I don't know."

When everyone had said *Your sister's having a baby,* I'd pictured her like that, just a baby, forever. I never thought about Addie getting older. But it was true, in a year my sister would have a toddler, and then a couple years after that she'd have a kindergartner.

"Think she'll be like you, or like me?"

"You mean, will she count her days by breakfasts or swims?"

"Maybe."

I separated all the rest of my tiny pieces of pizza. "Julia? How would you have counted your days? The breakfasts and swims, those are both Cassie things."

"Isn't everything Cassie-centric?"

"No. It really isn't." Nothing had been Cassie-centric for ages. "What's the Julia-centric counter for days?"

Julia thought. She thought and thought and thought. She twisted her pasta on her fork, and absentmindedly stripped another noodle and handed it to Addie.

"I don't even know. I don't know what I count them by, or even what I wish I counted them by."

"Did you used to know?"

"I guess I could have told you what I did in school. Or if I saw friends after school. I guess I could have told you how my week went, things like that. But counting nights I get up with Addie, or mornings I feel sleepy . . . those are all the same."

"Count how you woke up this week."

"Why?"

"I just want to hear what you say. Count."

"That first morning we left, I got up in the dark in my room, and got Addie ready as quietly as I could. The next morning, I woke up in your bed at the hotel. And the next morning, too, on the mountain? Then, what, the other hotel along the road, and then this morning at the bed-and-breakfast with you."

"That's something to count, if how you wake up affects your day."

"At home, it was the same every day, waking up with Addie, going back to sleep, waking up with Addie again. I guess a month ago there were days Mom or Dad woke me up to go to school. I maybe could have counted those, but I was so tired."

"Julia?"

She looked up.

"I can tell you my mornings, before we left. They were all the same, but . . . you put Addie on me. Every day. You never forgot, not since she was born. Maybe you didn't come to cuddle with me. But you brought her to. It must have mattered to you that she know me, even if, even if . . ."

Even if things had gone all funny between us.

She was still willing to cross the doorway into my room.

It was the closest we'd ever come to talking about it.

But we didn't. We stopped right there.

Though it hovered, out in the open.

We both knew it.

Something was nudging me, telling me to say I was sorry.

But I couldn't get out the words.

And Julia, the way she always did, was scooting us on past the moment to talk about things.

She had pulled out a wipe and was cleaning the sticky face and hands of her werebaby.

"How are you always so messy?" Julia asked.

"Goo," Addie said.

"She really is very cute," I said.

Julia looked up, and caught my eye.

"Thanks."

"I mean it," I said.

"So do I." She held my eyes with hers. "Thanks."

149

27

Mom and Dad had sat me down at the kitchen table.

"So are you finally going to tell me what's going on?" I asked.

"What's *going on*?" Mom asked.

"What do you think is going on?" Dad asked.

I sipped my ginger ale carefully. The taste reminded me of things you drink when your mouth already tastes like throw-up. The bubbles stung my tongue and nose.

"You're getting a divorce, aren't you?"

My parents both looked shocked.

"Why would you say that?" Mom asked.

"Because. Everyone's been all . . . upset. Fighting. There's nothing else it could be." I couldn't tell them how it felt when I saw them, all crying in a heap together as if I wasn't even a part of the family. I couldn't. Anyway, it had been over a month ago.

"No," Mom said. "Your father and I are *not* getting a divorce. But there is going to be a big change in our family."

"Someone's going away?" They were sending one of us away, I knew it. Me or Julia. Maybe she had been crying because it was her. Or because it was me. That would have been nice of her. To cry so much over me and then ignore me.

"Your imagination . . ." Dad shook his head. "Cassie, just listen for a minute. Your sister is going to have a baby."

"A what?"

"A baby."

"When?"

"In about five months."

"A *baby*?"

"Yes."

"With *Carter*?"

"Yes."

I bit my lip. I tried to take another sip of ginger ale, but it went down the wrong way and I started choking. Mom and Dad watched me sputter.

"So . . . Julia *is* going to leave."

"No, Julia is *not* going to leave. We already said that, no one is leaving. Your sister is young, and we want to keep her home with us. Her and her new baby."

"So you're going to be . . . *grandparents*? Aren't grandparents, like, old? Are you going to suddenly have gray hair and canes?"

"Cassie, this conversation is giving me more gray hairs right now." Mom ran her fingers along her scalp in exasperation.

"I didn't *ask* to have this conversation!"

They both stared at me.

Dad cleared his throat.

"We want you to be very understanding toward your sister. We want you to be supportive and helpful, okay?"

Wasn't this her fault? How hard was it *not* to do something?

Stupid Carter, why did she have to like him so much?

I wanted to throw my ginger ale in Dad's face, to show him just how much understanding I had.

But instead I pushed my chair back from the table. I thundered upstairs.

Julia was waiting for me in the doorway to her room.

"Cass?"

I looked her full in the face. I glared at her. And then, between us, I slammed the door to my room as hard as I could.

The slam cracked something. Something that sounded and looked and *felt* like a mirror. Or a stained glass window, maybe. Something that had been beautiful when it was whole.

The fragile thing broke.

Into a million, gazillion teeny, tiny pieces, and even if I tried every day, even if I crawled around on my hands and knees with a magnifying glass, I could never, ever find every single one and put it back together.

28

Julia woke up in a tangle with me, and when she saw me notice, she tapped my nose and climbed out of bed. She returned with a cooing Addie, complete with squishy morning diaper, and plopped her on my chest, just like every day.

"Hey, Addie-girl," I said.

Her eyes, big and blue, gazed into mine.

It was mostly the same crew at breakfast.

"Can I hold her?" asked the woman next to Julia.

"Sure." Julia handed Addie over.

The woman bounced Addie gently in her lap. Addie seemed to be okay with it. She didn't really get the Stranger Danger thing yet.

Did she think about Mom and Dad, or miss them? Did she think about Carter? Did she think about much of anything? She gave no sign that she missed anything.

One of the men poked his wife's arm, and then leaned in to whisper to her. She looked at us carefully, while he very carefully did *not* look at us. Then they looked back at each other, as if having a silent conversation.

Like Mom and Dad's eye-conversations.

A conversation about *us*.

My fruit salad suddenly tasted too sweet.

Upstairs in our room, Julia asked, "You okay?"

"Yeah, I . . . I just think I don't want to stay here anymore."

Julia looked at me, waiting. Finally she said, "We should move on anyway."

"No lumberjack," I said. "Where will we swim today?"

Julia looked thoughtful again and started packing.

I started collecting my things, too. "I'm running out of clean clothes."

"We are, too. Maybe we can stop at a Laundromat."

I'd never been to a Laundromat.

In the car, she handed me a pamphlet that she'd snagged on our way out.

"You're good at that." I turned it over. There were pictures of kids playing in shallow pools and sprinklers. "You can really spot them, even if we don't slow down on our way past."

"It won't be a swim, exactly. It's a water park. For little kids. I think you only pay for kids in the age range it's for, but older kids—like us—and babies are free. So maybe we'll have to buy like, one kid ticket, but it shouldn't cost a lot. Sound okay?"

"Yeah." It's amazing how even the idea of water calmed me down. Julia always found a way to include it in our day. She really did know me that well. "It will be fun to carry Addie through the sprinklers."

She was right about the tickets. At the counter, she said, "One kid."

The ticket lady looked at all of us and wasn't sure who the kid was meant to be. "Seven dollars," she said.

We had to change in the gross cement-floor open locker room, but it wasn't too bad.

There were *lots* of little kids running around, mostly two- and three- and four-year-olds.

"We should bring her back here, when she's older," I said.

"That would be fun, wouldn't it?"

But what was going to happen to us? Would the three of us still be together in two or three or four years?

It was hot out in the park, because it was all pavement, so you really wanted to be under those sprinklers. They had interesting shapes like sculptures or fantasy stuff like a mermaid lagoon and a pirate ship. Addie didn't care about any of that, but I thought it was neat. She didn't mind the sprinklers though. Eventually Julia took her off to the shade to eat, and I walked through the park, feeling like too big a kid to run around with the little ones.

The Laundromat had twenty washers and fifteen dryers, but we were the only people there.

We dragged in our bags. Julia set Addie's car seat on the floor and handed me a bunch of singles. "Turn these into quarters. It'll be fun. There's a machine over there."

I went to the change machine. It *was* fun. I put the dollars in one at a time and the quarters clattered out below. I stacked them in fours on a counter to make sure I'd gotten the right number of coins.

Julia had put all her and Addie's clothes into a big washer. I handed her the quarters.

"Put your things in. I'm going to get soap."

I unloaded my clothes right into the washer and shut it.

Julia came back, put in the quarters and the soap. Set some buttons and hit *Start*.

Then she put our towels and Addie's blankets into another washer and started that one, too.

"When did you learn how to do laundry?" I asked.

She looked at me for a minute, thinking. Like she was surprised I didn't know how to do laundry. "Actually, I guess after Addie. When she was really little, we must have made a whole hamper of dirty clothes every day. She was always spitting up or her diaper would leak." She looked down at Addie. "Why were you so messy?"

"Goo!"

We watched the clothes spin for a few minutes. You could see everything. The water got deeper and the soap made suds and the barrel turned and the clothes fell and swished around in a big heap, our things all mixed up. The dirt of our lives was being washed out together.

"I'm hungry," I said.

Julia handed me quarters and pointed. "Vending machine."

I picked peanut butter crackers and a bottle of water, and sat in the row of connected plastic chairs.

I turned my phone on. Finally decided to look at all those texts.

Bunches from Liana.

Where have you been?

Are you still swimming?

Did something happen?

Are you mad at us?

I thought. Texted back: I went on vacation with Julia and Addie.

Ate a couple more crackers.

Liana: You did!? You didn't say you were going! Where are you?

Me: Just driving around.

Liana: When will you be back?

Me: I don't know yet. How's practice?

Liana: Hard.

Several minutes went by.

I didn't know what else to say.

I was glad I was missing practice if it was hard.

But if I was missing hard practices, would I be any good?

I wished for that feeling of blood coursing through me, of trying to catch my breath, that followed a tough practice.

I checked the other texts. None from Piper. No surprises there.

But there were a few from Maya.

You guys good? Tell Julia I miss her.

Call me if you need anything.

Kiss those pudding cheeks for me.

LOL Addie's, I mean.

I smiled.

Julia had taken Addie out of her seat and was holding her in her lap a few chairs down. She was alternating reading her *Hippos Go Berserk!* and *Each Peach Pear Plum* over and over.

Our washers beeped and she handed me Addie. She put all our things in a metal cart and wheeled them to the dryers. I took over reading.

Then Julia was standing in front of me again. Beaming and holding a pamphlet.

I must have asked the question with my eyes, because she laughed and pointed to a display of them by the door.

I set down Addie's book and took the pamphlet.

"Campgrounds that also have cabins. Only four hundred for the whole week," Julia said. "What do you think?"

I looked up to see Julia's smile fading.

I was taking so long to answer.

Too long.

I looked back down.

"Oh," Julia said. She sat down next to me. Took Addie. "Hey . . . hey. Tell me."

"My first meet's in like ten days. Or it was supposed to be."

"That's important, Cass."

I shrugged. "It is. But it's not, like, the *most* important."

"What do you think is the most important?"

But I had answered her when I got in the car in the first place.

More important than fixing things with Mom and Dad.

More important than fixing things with Liana and Piper.

More important than my swim season.

"Let's go check it out," I said.

"Yeah?"

"Yeah. I want to."

The campgrounds were nice.

And there was a lake, which was great, of course.

Because most families wanted to camp in tents, or park their RVs, there were some cabins available. The cabins were set scattered among the trees not too far into the campgrounds, but a bit of a walk from the parking lot with all our stuff. They were sort of like hotel rooms all separate. Except that inside there was a little kitchenette. And sort of a damp smell.

Julia seemed happy though. She set down her things and started setting up the Pack 'n Play. I just dropped my duffel bag and sat on one of the beds.

"I know we went to the water park and our suits are all wet," Julia said, "but do you want to go to the lake? We can bring our towels to sit on."

"Sure."

She helped me get Addie strapped to my chest, and then dug out our towels.

There were other families at the sandy beach area of the lake and there were lifeguards, but, because it was kind of cloudy now, there weren't a lot of people swimming.

We spread our towels on the damp sand and settled to sit with our legs sticking straight out in front of us, our feet in the water.

Addie was snoozing on me, a puddle of drool starting to soak through my shirt. I didn't really mind. I made sure her little nose and mouth could get enough air. I brushed her soft hair back from her face.

Julia was looking at me with a very gentle expression.

Why?

The question hung there. Just above our toes peeking up on the surface of the lake. Just above the smooth water. In the little puffs of Addie's breath as she was sleeping. In the tips of our fingers, resting in the cold sand, not quite reaching for each other.

Finally Julia said, "I left because I wanted . . . just to . . . be myself a little, I guess." She drew her knees up to her chest, wrapping her arms around them, like she was trying to be as small as possible. Or like she felt small. "Just to . . . not have someone telling me what to do all day. To live my own life. I wasn't supposed to be home much longer. I was supposed to be going to college. Like all my friends are getting ready to do. And they're all working jobs this summer. And I'm doing *nothing*."

I looked out over Addie's head. "Taking care of Addie isn't nothing."

"But it's going nowhere."

"No, it isn't. It's going into a little girl. . . . And you finished high school."

"Barely."

"But you did. That was a really big thing."

"But it wasn't *supposed* to be a big thing. It was supposed to just be a regular thing."

Julia looked so defeated. My big, strong, beautiful sister, always ahead of me in everything. So far ahead and getting farther all the time. I couldn't catch up with her. I would *never* catch up with her. Eventually I would be so far behind her that it would be like we'd never been friends at all.

But she had picked me to run away with her.

Out of everyone.

And she picked me for Addie's middle name.

Out of all the names.

What did that *mean*?

The *why* was hanging in the air again. My turn.

To say why I was out here.

What I needed to fix.

"I miss you," I said.

"I'm right here. I've been right here, Cass."

"Then maybe it's my fault I missed you. I think I was jealous."

"Of what?"

"Everything was about you and Addie. What to do about you and Addie; how to get you through school, how to get you through a bad night. I was never a part of anything. There was Addie or there was Carter and I missed you so much I wanted you back just the way we were. I love Addie, I'm not saying I

161

don't. . . ." I felt Addie's sweet, sleepy body against me, trusting me, and I knew how true it was that I loved her. I looked over at Julia, who was waiting. "But I still want you to be my sister and not just Addie's mom."

She nodded. Her mouth was tight like maybe she had a lump in her throat. She looked out over the water.

"And you know all these . . . things I don't know. I feel like *you're* always moving ahead, learning these new things and getting these new people, and I'm the one who's always, always the same."

"Really?" She sounded surprised. "You're growing, too. Like you're a terrific auntie. You're always doing better at swimming and you have all these friends. You're moving up a grade. Which maybe didn't used to seem like a big deal, but now we know it is."

But only some of those things were true. I'd just run away from swimming. I didn't know if things were going to be okay with my friends. I didn't know how much I wanted them to be.

"Things seemed . . . different between us . . . after I was pregnant. Like you were so mad at me."

"Well, I guess, I had wanted *you* to tell me."

Julia was silent for a minute.

"You're right, I should have told you. I should have had the courage to tell you."

"It's *me*. Why would you need courage to tell me something?"

"It's a scary thing to say. I had to tell Mom and Dad because, well, I had to. But you . . . you had always looked up to me. Always thought I was perfect. I was about to throw all of that away. I was afraid of what you would think of me."

"Well, it was worse 'cause you didn't. I thought you didn't care enough for me to know. I thought Dad just told me because it was family business and I had to know because I lived in the house."

We were quiet again.

"I'm sorry," Julia said finally.

But I knew she was.

Because it was me she picked to come with her.

Because she hadn't wanted to leave me behind.

Because she'd given my name to the little baby in my lap.

Like, even though I was the little sister, there was room for her to look up to me, too.

29

We sat until Addie whimpered and stretched and woke and cried because she was hungry.

"My legs fell asleep! I can't get up!" I said.

Julia laughed and unbuckled the straps of the carrier. She lifted Addie to her and started to feed her.

"I'm going to go . . . over there." I pointed higher up the beach. "I want to take a nap farther from the water."

"Sure," Julia said. "Just don't leave the beach. Stay where you can see us. Where I can hear you if you call. Okay?"

"Yep."

I dragged my towel up the sand to the little ridge of grass under the trees. I lay down and stared up at the leaves and the gray clouds beyond them.

When I woke up, Julia was still sitting with Addie.

I walked down to the water at one end of the beach, went

in to just above my ankles. The sand at the bottom was thick and smooth, full of clay. Nice on the toes.

I headed toward Julia. She and Addie were both laughing. Then Julia pulled Addie close against her, and hugged her tight, for a long time.

Like Addie was the only person in the world.

Instead of going to them, I went back to my own towel.

Took my phone from my pocket.

Tapped Dad's name.

It rang, but only for a second.

"Hi Cassie."

He didn't sound mad.

"Dad?"

"Yes, honey. . . . Go ahead."

"I think I'm ready to come home."

30

Julia wasn't.

You'd be surprised how far you can get driving around aimlessly for six to eight hours a day over the course of a week.

Julia had to take me to an airport.

I'd never flown alone before.

I was a minor, so that was complicated.

Dad bought me the ticket with the airline on the phone. And explained to them that I would be alone so I got a special badge and there would always be a flight attendant nearby to help me.

Julia got a special badge, too, and she and Addie got to come to the gate with me.

So Julia was officially my adult to my being a minor. I giggled at how the airline was treating her as my special grown-up safe person, when they didn't know that actually she was my kidnapper because she had taken me away from my parents without asking them. Julia looked at me sideways, but maybe she understood; she shook her head and put a hand on my shoulder.

We looked out the window at my plane. It wasn't big, because we were in the middle of nowhere at a small airport.

I turned to Julia.

"Just, if you do ever want to come home, make sure you count ahead the days of driving and the gas money."

"Yes, Mom," she said.

"And I'll get birthday money this summer I could send you, if you tell me where."

"Yes, Mom."

"And don't order the lumberjack. It's too much food. You don't need all that food by yourself."

"Yes, Mom."

"And—" My voice caught. "Please come back?"

"Yes, Mom!" But she looked more serious. "I promise I will." She raised her right hand. "Lumberjack's honor."

"Julia? I'm sorry, too."

"I know."

"And . . . Julia?"

"Yeah, dummy?"

"I love you."

"And I love you. I love you so much, you'll never even figure it out."

But I had.

I had all the reasons.

We held each other for a long time.

"Cassie Applegate?" asked a flight attendant. "It's time to board."

I nodded and let go of Julia.

I picked up my duffel bag and saluted.

Julia saluted back.

I pinched Addie's bare toes and kissed her cheeks. "Bye for now, love bug."

What I really wanted to do was squeeze her and squeeze her.

How much was I going to miss? How fast did babies grow? What if she got another tooth? What if she started crawling?

I kissed her toes, too.

And then I went to the doorway of the gate. I waved, and Julia waved back and blew kisses. She was crying, but she looked happy.

And then I was off, headed home, by myself.

But I felt less by myself than I had in a long time.

Being in the same place had nothing to do with us being there for each other.

As I found my seat, I thought how I was doing something that Julia had never done, flying in an airplane alone, and how even though we were going to be apart for a little bit, I felt closer and closer to her as the plane left the ground.

And I knew that when I got home, Mom and Dad would be happy to see me.

Even if we had to work some things out. Even if there was some yelling and I was in trouble.

I knew they would hold me against them the way Julia had held Addie.

31

The plane had maybe like thirty rows of four. They sat me right in the front. Nobody was sitting next to me. I stared out the window while there was something to see, and then it got dark. Sometimes there was another airplane zooming off to someplace else. We weren't the only ones in the sky.

Once the flight had gotten off the ground, and the flight attendants had handed out drinks, one of them came back to talk to me.

"Can I get you anything else?" she asked.

"No, I'm good." I turned back to the window.

She stayed, watching me.

No book.

Dead phone.

Nothing to do.

Nothing to do but think about what my parents were going to say.

The flight attendant sat down in the empty seat next to me.

She didn't look that much older than Julia. "I'm Jen. You can let me know if you do need anything, okay?"

I nodded.

"Are you heading to or returning from?"

"Going home."

"Were you visiting family?"

"Not exactly. I mean, I was with family. My sister. We ran away."

Jen looked surprised. And worried, like suddenly the small talk was over.

"Are you okay?"

"Yeah. . . ." I thought about it harder. "Yeah, I'm okay."

"And your sister is okay?"

"Yeah. She's great."

"You must have gotten pretty far if you have to fly home."

I nodded again.

"Did you have dinner?"

I shook my head.

"We have these little sandwich boxes. Do you want one?"

"I don't have any money."

"I can comp you one. I'll be right back."

She brought another little can of Sprite and a small cardboard box. Inside was a turkey-and-cheese sandwich, a couple condiment packets, a little bag of potato chips, and a cookie in a wrapper.

"Thanks."

She sat in the empty seat again. I was about halfway through the sandwich when she said, "I ran away once. I only made it about three hours. I just went down the road to the woods, set up a little camp with sticks and my raincoat, in case it rained. It didn't. I brought a whole loaf of peanut butter and jelly."

"A loaf?"

"Yeah." She laughed. "Like I took a whole loaf of bread, made PB&Js, and put them all back into the bread bag."

"How old were you?"

"I don't know, nine maybe. I thought I could live on that for a few months. By then I would have made enough arrows that I could hunt deer. I think I made five arrows or so in the three hours."

"Why did you go back?"

"To see if people had noticed I'd gone. They hadn't. I was always playing outside."

"What did you do with all the sandwiches?"

"My brother and sister ate them during their Monopoly marathon. My brother always won. They never let me play." She sat for a moment, remembering, and I finished my sandwich. "So . . . everything okay at home?"

I thought about it as I unwrapped my dessert.

Probably a lot of other kids did have it bad at home. Like they weren't safe there. That was probably what she was asking.

"Yeah."

Jen was quiet, but didn't get up. Like she was waiting for me to think through why I had left, even though it didn't seem like she thought I would tell her. I was going to have to talk to Mom and Dad about it in an hour anyway.

I put all the empty wrappers and bags and soda cans into the cardboard box.

"I'll take that for you," Jen said, back to her flight attendant voice. She stood up and moved to the aisle. "When we land, sit tight, and I'll take you to meet your parents at the gate."

When we started our descent, I could see things again, the even night-lights of suburbia. Was one of the lights my house, or was ours dark because my parents were coming to get me?

It was a little bumpy on the way down.

32

And there they were, standing right by the rope at the gate.

Mom's hair in a sloppy ponytail. She never wore it like that. Purple circles under her eyes.

Dad also looked worried, but when he saw me, a hint of a relieved smile came to his lips.

Jen took her hand off my upper back, where she had placed it to steer me through the other passengers. She lifted the lanyard for the unaccompanied-minor ID badge from around my neck.

"Good luck," she said.

I ran.

Past the rope and right at Mom.

Wrapped my arms around her middle. Hers wrapped around me. And then Dad's around both of us.

When we broke apart, the *why* was there again.

Even though it was after ten at night, there was a restaurant still open in the airport. Dad asked for a table for three and we sat down.

"Maybe you want to get a sundae or something?" Dad asked. "We never did get out to celebrate your report card."

"I don't know if I feel like it."

But when the waiter came, Dad ordered waffles with strawberries and whipped cream, and, for me, a brownie fudge sundae.

When the waiter had walked away, Dad said, "Not to decide for you. You can ask for something else, too, if that's not what you want. . . . I just know you like them."

I did like them.

Dad was trying to show he was listening, on two counts.

I looked from one to the other. They were both looking steadily back at me.

No eye-conversations without me.

They looked almost a little afraid, like they didn't want to say or do the wrong thing and have me get upset.

Finally Mom said, "What happened?"

"I was invisible."

They both waited.

"You stopped coming to my swim meets. I missed so much last year. You never asked if I minded. You didn't notice or care that Piper and Liana don't come over anymore. I don't even know if they're still my friends. But I'm sure you don't care about that, either."

Mom's eyes were getting watery. "Of course we do. I'm so, so sorry."

I looked at Dad instead. "You didn't care about anything until that stupid science grade."

"I'm sorry. I should have been paying attention to the other stuff, too," Dad said. "I wish you would have told us about all those things that were bothering you. We can't know if you don't tell us. But maybe you wanted to and we weren't listening, or weren't making you feel like we would listen. Maybe we should have asked more."

The waiter set our food on the table.

I wasn't sure how much I wanted to act like the sundae was just right, so I took just a small bite. But it was really good, and I went back for a bigger one.

Dad hadn't touched his waffles yet. He was looking at me.

Finally I said, "I don't want to tell you everything. I don't want your help with everything. I just want to feel more like . . . sometimes . . . the day I'm having is important, too. Like, the day I'm actually having. Not the one you want me to have."

They both nodded like this made sense.

Dad picked up his knife and fork, but put them back down. Then he lifted his plate, offering it to me. I scooped off a whole bunch of strawberries and added them to my sundae.

"Thank you for explaining all that," Mom said.

We all started eating.

Dad was right, the sundae made me happy.

And they didn't ask me to explain about or for Julia.

They let the three of us, for once, be just that—the three of us.

33

I woke up in the morning surprised by how bright and quiet and still it was. I rolled over. I stretched. I stared at my ceiling.

It was the first morning in months I had woken up on my own, when my body just felt like it was time to get up.

I missed Addie's weight on me.

I missed Julia. Wanting to see me, to include me.

But this was going to be my own day, one of my own invention.

A Cassie-centric kind of day.

It didn't last very long.

First of all, it was noon.

Second, when I slid into a chair at the counter with my bowl of cereal, Dad said, "You're grounded."

"What?"

I looked between him and Mom.

"Uh-huh," she said from the sink.

"What does that even mean?" I'd never been grounded before. I figured it meant I had to stay home from social plans. I didn't *want* to see my friends just yet, but I would have to see them a little at practice anyway.

"No friends. No phone. No swimming."

"No *swimming*? For how long?"

"Two days."

"What? I'll never catch up!"

"You didn't seem to be worried about that when you took off for a week without telling us," Dad said.

Ouch. Good one. I winced.

"Two days," Mom agreed. "We can spend the time together."

She grinned. With extra emphasis.

"Got it," I said.

"Phone." Dad held out his hand.

"It's charging." I pointed. "But can't I just text Liana to say I'm back? Please? Even prisoners get one phone call."

After a brief eye-conversation with Dad, Mom said, "Okay."

I quickly texted Liana: I'm home. Can't swim today or tomorrow but I'll be back the next day.

I returned to my cereal, which was getting soggy, and stirred it around.

My phone pinged.

All three of us looked at each other. Mom shook her head

at me and went over to check it. "She says, 'Good, that's time trials!'"

"What?" I leapt to my feet. "I'm going to go to time trials without practicing almost at all?" I slumped back into my chair.

"Don't worry," Dad said. "We won't let you be out of shape. We've made a list of feats of strength that need doing in the yard."

He slid me a sheet of paper with writing *all over* it. I gagged at the word *mulch*. Dad grinned. With super-extra emphasis.

I glared at him.

Mom came over from the sink and kissed me on the head. When she'd walked away, I tried to go back to my cereal. Such a boring breakfast after the great ones on vacation.

"I'm turning your phone off now," Mom said.

"Wait!" I said. They both looked at me. "I mean . . . you could do it from yours. But tell Julia it will be off. In case she needs something. She should know."

They both nodded.

"I'll do it now," Dad said. He took out his phone for a minute. "There." He put the phone back in his pocket.

The three of us went still.

The house was so, so quiet.

Finally, looking into my bowl of disintegrated cereal, I said, "We got the lumberjack every day. Well, most days."

Both Mom and Dad looked interested. They had heard almost nothing about the trip. About what their girls did together when they spontaneously set off into the world.

Mom looked thoughtful. "The closest thing to a lumberjack available at Chez Applegate is eggs. You can make your own toast."

"Deal."

"Scrambled?"

"Over easy . . . please."

34

My head felt woozy and my throat scratchy as I packed my swim bag.

I shouldn't have been nervous for time trials.

Maybe it was because I'd missed so much?

Had to face Piper and Liana?

I refolded my towel and stuffed it into my bag, zipped it slowly.

I was going to do fine. It was better than not showing up again. Maybe I'd have to have bad lanes for a couple meets until I got my times down.

I sat down on the bench by the door in the mudroom and buried my face in my hands.

Mom came to make sure I was ready.

"Oh, Cassie . . . you don't look good."

"I'm fine." I stood up and wobbled. I tried to swallow but my throat was still scratchy.

"Sit." Mom put her hands on my face.

Dad showed up, took his keys off the hook. "Ready?" But then he turned around and saw us. "Uh-oh. Thermometer?"

Mom nodded.

"I can't miss it," I said.

"We'll see, honey. If you're sick . . ."

Dad stuck the thermometer in my mouth and we waited. It beeped; Dad took it back and checked. "One hundred two. Tylenol and bed."

Later, my bedroom door creaked open.

"Cassie?"

"Liana?"

I peeked at the doorway.

"I came to see if you were okay. I mean, you must not be, to miss time trials, but I mean, I came to see if you were upset."

"Oh. Thanks. I was. Now I feel too icky."

She held out a bakery box. "So . . . you probably don't want these?"

Cupcakes. Four of them. With letters frosted across: *Get Well Cas sie.*

"Not right now."

"I'll help. You can have one tomorrow."

"Liana . . . what are you doing here? I mean, your mom . . ."

"I told her it wasn't contagious."

"Um, today it probably is contagious."

Liana laughed. "I don't mean that." She pulled my desk

chair into the opposite corner, as far away from my bed as she could get it, sat down, and started unwrapping a cupcake.

"Did you really tell her that?"

She laughed. "No. I told her you are my friend and I missed you. That you didn't do anything wrong. That what happened to Julia had nothing to do with you. When you weren't at time trials, I told her I wasn't waiting another day to be your friend again. She said okay, I was right, and she took me to pick out something for you and dropped me off. She doesn't want me to get sick, though, so I have to stay far away and she's coming back in forty-five minutes."

I sank into my pillow, cozy but nauseous. Then I sat up.

"Liana! What about *your* time trials?"

She laughed again as she started on her second cupcake. "That was another whole thing. I worked it out, though. Coach will get both our times in a couple days."

I lay back down and stared at the ceiling. "It's not the same, to get them separate. It's not a race."

"It will be. That's how I got permission. We'll race each other. I mean, you'll probably be ahead, but still, it's better than by yourself. And who knows, maybe *'cause you missed a week of practice,* I can kick your sorry butt."

"Keep eating those cupcakes." I rolled over to try to get more comfy.

Liana licked her fingers. "I left you the ones with your name. So when you eat them, you will just be Cassie, already well."

"Thanks."

The fan whirred and whirred and blew the hot off me.

"Where's Piper?"

"Piper wouldn't miss time trials for a million dollars."

But Liana would.

Liana would miss them for me.

"She's probably hoping to get ahead of you this summer," Liana said.

It was the best and worst thing about swimming—having to be competitive with your own teammates.

"Liana?"

"Yeah?"

"Find out what she got today. When I'm back, let's both beat her."

"Deal."

35

In the morning, my fever was gone. Which got me out of a trip to the doctor, but both Mom and Dad agreed I couldn't go back to swimming yet.

Which made the day mostly boring.

They let me sit on the back deck, under the umbrella. I brought the cupcakes with me and ate them slowly. C-a-s, s-i-e.

"You sure cupcakes are a good idea?" Mom asked.

"Yeth," I said with my mouth full. I swallowed. "I never threw up."

Dad sat next to me and held up a deck of Uno cards. I nodded, and he started shuffling.

"Do you think Julia and Addie got sick?" I asked.

"It's easy to pick up a bug while you're traveling, but maybe you caught it on the airplane."

I texted Julia: I got sick. Did you guys?

Dad and I had played a couple hands by the time she texted back: We didn't! All good here. Feel better. <3

Dad watched me read, so I told him, "They're okay."

"Good. . . . Thanks."

After I beat him again, he said, "Your birthday's coming up. How do you want to celebrate?"

It would be weird to have my birthday without Julia. If she wasn't back by then.

"Just a cake, I guess."

My birthday always meant that school was around the corner.

"Can you take me to the art store? I need to pick out a scrapbook or something for my journal for Mr. Connelly."

"Now? Are you too tired?"

"I'm not too tired."

At the store, I wandered the aisles, Dad trailing behind me with a basket.

I looked at journals. Scrapbooks. Sketchbooks.

Nothing seemed right.

So I wandered farther than I'd meant to.

I came home with a wooden box with a latch and key, paintbrushes, acrylic paints, and a small mirror.

"That's not a journal," Mom said when I spread everything out on newspaper on the dining room table.

"Of course it is," I said.

I painted the outside of the box periwinkle. On the inside of the lid, I glued the mirror and, in multicolor, I painted, "A Journal by Cassie Applegate."

The next day, when the box was dry, I took it up to the desk in my room. I filled it with photos and medals I took off my bulletin board. I took the photo of Addie from the back of Julia's journal, and a couple photos of us from when we were little. I could put them back later.

Then I got out a stack of fresh lined paper and also some colored stationery pages.

And I wrote.

I wrote about all my swims from my trip with Julia, each on a separate sheet. I folded them up tiny, tiny, and threw them into the box.

I wrote about canoeing with Dad at the lake, folded it up, and tossed it into the box.

I wrote about the day I met Addie. I wrote about waiting for Addie. About feeling her kick in Julia's stomach and teaching her to kick in the pool. About her waking me up in the morning and saying good night to her at bedtime.

I wrote about my best swim meets, and my worst swim meets.

I wrote about Liana and Piper. I added my broken anklet to the box.

I searched for the hide-and-seek numbers Julia had given me, and threw in the ones that had been savable. I wrote about our game.

I wrote about eating oranges in Julia's lap so long ago the memory was fuzzy. On a different sheet of paper, I wrote about picturing the other little girl who would sit in her lap.

I wrote about flying by myself.

When the box was stuffed, I stirred everything that was inside.

Why should my journal be in order when life didn't always seem to be?

36

A few days later, I spotted my name on the pile of mail in the hall.

A bright yellow envelope. The postmark was smudged. No return address.

I opened it.

It was a birthday card. Sort of the opposite of a belated birthday card. The front said, "Happy Almost-Birthday!"

No one had signed the inside.

Instead, there was a small, flat card.

It said:

13

37

It wasn't hot enough for the air conditioner that night.

Which is why I'd been sleeping with my window open.

Which is why I heard the car.

It pulled up close and its engine turned off.

I flew downstairs and out onto the front lawn in my bare feet and pajamas.

And then I was in her arms, and she was spinning me.

"Julia . . . Julia . . ."

"Fourteen . . . fifteen . . . sixteen . . ."

She stopped spinning us. I put my finger to her lips.

"You're right," she said. "No rush."

"No," I said.

We were always hiding, always seeking.

Always finding.

"Addie?"

"In the car, silly. Sleeping."

Lights had come on in the house. Two silhouettes stood in the doorway.

Julia glanced at them, then back at me.

"I'll get her," I said.

"You sure?"

"Yeah, you go."

She paused. "They mad?"

"Um . . ." I bit my lip. "Your bed is made. And Addie's. Always ready for you."

Julia let out a long breath. "That's good. Thanks."

I squeezed her again, tight. "Welcome home."

When I let her go, she headed to the front door.

I went to the car.

Addie.

Sound asleep, drooling, head tipped to the side.

Looking bigger, even though it hadn't even been two weeks.

I unbuckled her carefully, eased her out, and rested her head on my shoulder.

"There, Addie-girl, it's okay. You're home."

She stretched and squirmed against me.

"Don't wake up. Shhh . . . shhh . . . shhh."

Did she remember our house? Did she remember me?

How long did babies remember things?

As I brought her inside, I blocked out the sound of Julia and our parents in the kitchen.

It was her night, not mine.

I'd already said what I needed to say.

It was her turn.

I woke to a weight on my chest, and little patting hands on my face.

"Morning, Cass."

I opened my eyes.

"Surprise." Julia lay down next to me on her side, blocking Addie from the edge.

Addie smiled and laughed. She shrieked and put her fingers in my eyes.

"You'll stay?" I asked Julia.

"Yep."

"You want to?"

"I do. I think things will be a little different now."

"Good."

I sat up and flipped Addie onto her back so I could tickle her stomach. Then I lay back down and settled her between me and Julia.

"Want to have a perfect day?"

Julia ran her finger down Addie's stomach. "I have to go to Carter's. I have to . . . explain. And he really needs to see Addie."

I nodded.

"But," she said, "want to have dinner tonight? Just the two of us?"

"Yeah."

"Good." She scooped up Addie and headed to the door. "Oh. I printed this for you." She set something on my desk.

After she'd shut the door, I got up and went to see what it was.

The picture of me and Addie at the waterfall.
I picked it up. And the little card that said *13*.
I looked at my painted journal-box.
Then I looked at my almost-bare bulletin board.
Ready to start over with the new layers of my life.
I tacked both to my bulletin board. Stood back. And smiled.

*T*he end of the summer. Regional championships.

I stood behind my lane, waiting for the last heat before mine to finish.

I read the heat and lane Sharpie'd on my arm again, just to make sure.

I was in the right place.

I had a good entry time, so I had a middle lane.

I suctioned my goggles again, just to make sure.

Straightened my suit straps.

Shook my arms.

Hopped.

Just to make sure.

Top eight would swim again tonight. For medals.

I looked down the row of starting blocks; Liana was waving at me. She was in my heat, in an outside lane.

I waved back.

It was nice to know I would have a friend in the water. Even though I would race just *me* alone.

Piper, who had already swum, was outside the fence, wrapped in her towel. Watching to cheer us, but also to see if her time would hold for the top eight.

And there were Mom and Dad, having moved to the fence for my race.

And in the stands behind them, Julia with Addie on her lap, Julia's hand waving Addie's. Even though I knew Addie couldn't recognize me from so far away in my cap and goggles.

I wouldn't see them from the water.

I wouldn't need to.

Here or not, I knew they were always cheering for me.

Even if my race was just me alone.

The water was cleared.

"Step up."

I looked all the way to the end of my lane and back.

I was going to seek out my own perfect.

I got this.

"Swimmers, take your marks. . . ."

ACKNOWLEDGMENTS

I would like to acknowledge the existence of my siblings, Bean, Bobbie, and Alex.

I owe a special note of thanks to Bobbie and Alex, who gave me permission to borrow their game of counting to thirty very, very slowly.

They have been counting since 1999.

Alex?

Bobbie says:

19

ABOUT THE AUTHOR

Suzanne LaFleur grew up with her three younger siblings. They went swimming every day. Now they live up and down the East Coast and team up for road trips home to Mom and Dad. She is the author of *Love, Aubrey; Eight Keys; Listening for Lucca; Beautiful Blue World;* and *Threads of Blue.* She lives in New York City. Visit her online at suzannelafleur.com, and follow her on Facebook at Suzanne LaFleur Author.